SOUL CITY

ALSO BY TOURÉ

The Portable Promised Land

SOUL CITY

A

NOVEL

TOURÉ

PICADOR

NEW YORK

SOUL CITY. Copyright © 2004 by Touré. All rights reserved. Printed in the United States of America. No part of this book may be used or reproduced in any manner whatsoever without written permission except in the case of brief quotations embodied in critical articles or reviews. For information, address Picador, 175 Fifth Avenue, New York, N.Y. 10010.

www.picadorusa.com

Picador® is a U.S. registered trademark and
is used by St. Martin's Press under license from Pan Books Limited.

For information on Picador Reading Group Guides, as well as ordering,
please contact Picador.
Phone: 646-307-5626
Fax: 212-253-9627
E-mail: readinggroupguides@picadorusa.com

Book design by Jo Anne Metsch

Library of Congress Cataloging-in-Publication Data

Touré.
Soul City : a novel / Touré.
p. cm.
ISBN 0-312-42516-3
EAN 978-0-312-42516-6
1. African Americans—Fiction. 2. Utopias—Fiction. I. Title.

PS3570.O768S68 2004
813'.6—dc22   2004001415

First published in the United States by Little, Brown and Company,
a division of Time Warner Book Group

First Picador Edition: September 2005

10 9 8 7 6 5 4 3 2 1

SOUL CITY

A map of the world that does not include Utopia is not worth even glancing at.

— *Oscar Wilde*

1

T HE TRAIN eased to a stop at Soul City, and Cadillac
Jackson smoothed off into a new life. He had a pen in
one hand and a pad in the other, hungry to catch every detail.
He was from The City and infused with the requisite tower-
ing ambition that everyone from The City had. He'd come to
Soul City to research the book that would establish him as one
of the great writers of his generation. Whether he had the tal-
ent to render the world of Soul City honestly remained to be
seen. He'd been sent by *Chocolate City Magazine,* ordered to
spend three days, write a short piece about the mayoral election, and get back home. But he had other plans. He'd always
wanted to visit the city that boasted "more mojo than any city
in the world." To see the world-famous one-hundred-foot-tall
Afro Pick, to hear one of Revren Lil' Mo Love's crazy sermons,
to get a sack of six at the Biscuit Shop. And he'd always wanted

to write a book about Soul City. He knew all the other books had gotten it wrong. No one had really figured out what made Soul City what it was. He vowed not to leave until he knew. Great books had been inspired by Dublin, Venice, Paris, Bombay, and New York. He would add Soul City.

Cadillac stepped out of the station onto Groove Street and saw men cooling down the block with walks of such visible rhythm, physical artistry, and attention to aesthetics that it looked like a pimp-stroll convention. Across the street a barber was clipping and snipping at a prodigious fro in an open-air barbershop, clipping with the arrogance of a famous painter wielding his brush, snipping whether in or out of the fro, turning those scissors into a snare. On the corner a street sweeper swept with a theatricality that transformed his duty into modern dance.

On Mojo Road a flock of girls double-dutched, pigtails bouncing, the rope cracking at lightning speed, while the three in the middle danced in the air, never touching the ground. They seemed to be levitating, but those ropes were moving so fast it was difficult to tell exactly what was going on. Maybe the ropes were whipping up a mini–sonic boom that created a pocket of air that the girls could surf for a moment, like an invisible magic carpet. That made no sense. But what he saw made no sense either: six- and seven-year-old girls in rainbow-colored tights with ropes zipping under their bent legs eight, nine, ten times before they touched the sidewalk. They touched down less from gravity than from boredom, as if they'd been just hanging out in the air.

He checked into his hotel, the Copasetic on Cool Street, then walked from Nappy Lane to Gravy Ave to Cornbread Boulevard. The sidewalks were forty to fifty feet wide and the streets were abuzz with all-age minifestivals of hair braiding, marble shooting, bubble blowing, puddle stomping, roller-skating, faithful preaching, "God's coming!," mommies strolling, babies toddling, groceries spilling, lots of flirting, and gossip flying. On Bookoo Boulevard the Vinylmobile crept by, offering old albums for a few dollars, and children poured from homes to chase it as children elsewhere chase ice cream trucks. The Washeteria on Badass Ave had its own DJ so you could dance while you dried. And it made perfect sense that in a world where bad means good, the traffic signals used green for stop and red for go.

On Irie Way and Downhome Drive he found flowers leaping up through the sidewalks. They were American beauties and African violets, more vibrant, fragrant, and giant than any he'd ever seen. He bent and saw their roots were buried beneath the concrete. The flowers had confronted the pavement and punched through it, undeterrable in their desire to get closer to the sun. Bent low, he could see the little speakers that had been built into the sidewalks all over town. First he heard Satchmo think to himself what a wonderful world, then Bob spoke of redemption songs, then James proclaimed he was Black and he was proud. There was an easy vibe to the place, as if everything in the world were possible and there was all the time in the world to do it, for Soul City minutes were ninety seconds long. Cadillac tried to scribble a few words that would capture the scene, but nothing came.

2

A T THE corner of Ebony and Mecca, Cadillac found the
Biscuit Shop. He knew they had supernaturally good
biscuits. He didn't know they had a DJ and people danced as
they ate their biscuits. When he walked in, Prince was talking
about a lady cabdriver and there was a full-blown party goin on
even though, or maybe because, it was Friday afternoon. Someone screamed that the roof was on fire, and a couple jumped up
on top of a table to dance. An ancient-looking woman came
trembling from behind the counter, her pace so much slower
than the high-slung rhythm of the party that she seemed like a
superimposed freeze-frame. She was golden brown and paper-
thin with silvery hair and Coke-bottle glasses, leaning for dear
life on an ornately carved cane, a thick wool shawl clinging to
her shoulders. She looked as sweet as any cookie-bakin grandmother who ever lived. Then she opened her mouth. "Git the
fuck down from there!" she croaked. "Y'all think y'all at home?"

"Sorry, Granmama," they said, their heads bowed. They jumped down. But the party went on.

As Cadillac waited in line he looked at the photos that covered the walls. There was Granmama with Dizzy Gillespie and Charlie Parker, the men young, sweaty, and clearly brimming with thoughts. There was Granmama beside Martin Luther King, Ralph Ellison, Langston Hughes, Marcus Garvey, Zora Neale Hurston, Josephine Baker, Madame CJ Walker. And sepia photos and daguerreotypes of Granmama beside people who had been dead for a good long while: Frederick Douglass, Phyllis Wheatley, Sojourner Truth, Harriet Tubman. For these pictures to be real, he thought, Granmama would have to be more than two hundred years old. They had to be Photoshopped. A two-hundred-year-old woman was impossible.

When Cadillac sat down with his sack of six biscuits, they were still piping hot and the butter's seductive scent was dancing into his nose. As soon as he took a bite the biscuit began melting in his mouth, first flaking into pieces, then a little river of butter washing over his tongue, butter sweeter than he'd ever tasted. He remembered that it was just the sort of biscuit his aunt Omen had given him at her house on Downhome Drive when he was a boy. The taste of it shook an image loose from the ocean floor of his memory. It came floating up toward his consciousness, the memory of what it was to have been young and in the air, riding on breezes, cutting through clouds, flying. There was no need to put his arms out because gliding was as natural as walking. The weight of life was lifted and the air felt slower and he felt free. He gazed down at Soul City from a bird's view and saw Honeypot Hill and Niggatown and Soul City's central monument, its Eiffel Tower, the one-hundred-foot-tall black steel Black fist Afro Pick, with fifty-foot-tall teeth shooting up from the ground and flowing together to form a muscular, militant Black power fist, so big that aliens cruising by in outer space couldn't miss it. Then everything stopped. How could he remember flying if he'd never flown in his life? How could he remember the Afro Pick if he'd never seen it? And who was this Aunt Omen person? *What was in this biscuit?* It was a long time before Cadillac understood that each of Granmama's biscuits had a memory baked into it, but a memory from whoever had baked that biscuit. He'd gotten lucky and eaten that one in a thousand baked by the one girl who worked in the shop and knew how to fly.

When Cadillac stood to leave, the DJ scratched and suddenly Prince's needle-sharp falsetto leaped from the speakers, wanting your extra time and your . . . kiss. The Biscuit Shop screamed as one and launched into dancing so intense that the room was just this side of a riot. He looked at the DJ in her dowdy Biscuit Shop uniform, dull gray like a cheap maid's outfit. But she had long, cascading diva curls, a face like Dorothy Dandridge, and was flowing from vinyl to vinyl with a cigarette in her hand. Her name tag said MAHOGANY. When he passed she didn't smile. He walked to his hotel replaying the memory of flight over and again, clinging to the images, afraid if he forgot for a moment he'd never know flight again.

3

———

BY MIDNIGHT that Friday there were thousands in Paradise Park munching on blackened barbeque chicken and gulping beer from peanut butter jars, ready to cheer for their candidate in the Soul City mayoral debate, sponsored by the Biscuit Shop. Cadillac thought it was an hour more congruous with partying than politics, but he had a wing in one hand and a pen in the other, and he was about to learn that in Soul City, how you party is very political.

The mayor of Soul City was Emperor Jones, a six-foot-three, 330 pound, seventy-two-year-old man in a three-piece, deep blue, white chalk pinstripe suit. The gold links of his pocket-watch made a line as long as a normal man's arm. A leonine mane of graying curls ringed his face. He'd been the mayor of Soul City for twelve long years, and this year would be his last. Four decades back he made a name for himself in Soul City when he won the Nut-Holding Contest in the Summertime Carnival. The Nut-Holding Contest required men merely to stand holding their nuts as long as possible. Emperor stood there six days, fourteen hours, and twenty-eight minutes straight, sometimes sleeping while standing and holding his nuts. His record still stands. They put his picture in the *Soul City Defender* and in no time flat he was campaigning for city council. Now, after six consecutive terms as mayor, he was at the end of a life in public service, and Soul City was about to start over with a new, and undoubtedly lesser, man. As Emperor stepped to the podium they chanted, "Don't Go!" so loud it seemed certain he would've been reelected the moment he agreed to run. He wanted to run, but the stress of being the mayor of Soul City had made it impossible to lose the weight that his doctors and girlfriends were on him about.

In Soul City the mayor's prime function is to DJ for the town. All the speakers in all the sidewalks are connected back to the central turntable at the mayor's mansion, and every two years the people go to the polls and choose a mayor based on what he plans to spin while in office.

This year's ballot consisted of the Jazz Party's Coltrane Jones, the Hiphop Nation's Willie Bobo, and the Soul Music Party's Cool Spreadlove. Emperor Jones, of the Independent Party, had the DJ skills and the taste to integrate a variety of sounds and create a balanced playlist. The candidates had neither the vision nor the ears to get beyond their party's narrow platform. Whoever won would stick to the music of his party alone, which could unbalance the mood of the town and lead to all sorts of catastrophes. It was a critical point in Soul City history.

Everyone wanted to know who Emperor thought should be the next mayor, but Emperor looked at all three candidates with disgust. He refused to endorse any of them. They all made him cringe for the future of Soul City. Especially Cool Spread-love. Who was now an hour late.

"I'm gonna open this evening's festivities," Emperor Jones boomed into the microphone, "with a thank ya to our sponsor!" He turned to look for Granmama and from behind him she trembled into view, her soft droopy skin shaking with each careful step. Her smile was brief and reluctant, but the entire park bloomed at the sight of her dentures like a valley of flowers rising to attention when the sun comes up over the horizon.

"Granmama been sponsoring the mayoral debates for one hundred forty-four years now!"

"One hundred forty-two!" Granmama said, annoyed. "Get it right, kiddo."

"So we got to keep supportin Granmama! She *is* Soul City!" The Soulful cheered.

"Y'all know her Biscuit Shop at the corner of Ebony and Mecca. Go down there and get a sack of six of Granmama's soft, flaky butter-baked-in biscuits! They so light and flaky if there's anything left to swallow after ya finished chewing . . ."

The crowd answered as one, "YOUR NEXT BISCUIT'S FREE!"

"Granmama," the mayor said, "think this'll be the year you finally get around to putting cornbread on the menu like you been talkin bout?"

"I don't know," Granmama grumbled dismissively. "It's hard as shit gittin the biscuits right."

"For the last time," he whispered, *"no cursing onstage!"*

"Fuck you, fatboy," she whispered.

An aide rushed up. "She doesn't obey Death," the aide whispered. "Why would she obey you?" The aide gently coaxed her off the stage. The mayor ripped a hanky from his pocket and dabbed his sweaty brow. "In all my years in Soul City," he said grimly, "this is the most important election I've ever seen. You may think this is about music, but it's not. It's about character. The character of this very city. A couple years with just one sound on the speakers and we're going to become a completely different city!"

A muffled grumble came from the Soulful. It was nearing one in the morning. They were eager for the music to start. They loved Emperor, but in everything he did he went on forever, from holding his nuts for days to being mayor for years to speechifying for hours when it was least wanted. "When I was a boy," he said, "my grandmother used to say, 'Sound'll shape ya!' What she meant was music is just like food! You are what you eat, and what you hear makes you what you are. On Monday, when you go to the polls, don't think about what you want to hear, think of who you want to be and who you don't wanna be because —"

"Enough with the gum-flappin, fatboy!" Granmama yelled, turtling her way toward him. "We wanna hear some fuckin music!"

Emperor Jones cut his eyes at her but said nothing. Even a man as powerful as Emperor dared not talk back to Granmama in public. He walked over to a set of turntables and a mixer, took a power cord from the hands of a smiling aide, and as photographers from the *Soul City Defender* and the *Soul City Inquirer* snapped away, he plugged the cord into the base of a street lamp. "I declare the debate begun!" The Soulful cheered wildly. Emperor looked down the stage and saw that Cool Spreadlove still had not arrived. He was now more than two hours late. Emperor shook his head in disgust.

First to the turntables was Coltrane Jones, sporting a chocolate brown suit with sharp black wing tips and a black beret tilting off his shaved and gleaming dome. He flicked on the mixer, pulled the sonic earmuffs over his beret, and spun through a history of jazz.

Once, the Jazz Party had ruled Soul City. In the 40s, 50s, and early 60s, they'd dominated even more completely than the Blues Party had before them or the Gospel Party, who prefer to be called God's Party, had before them. In the mid-60s the Soul Music Party took control of the mayor's mansion and stayed there throughout the 70s, so powerful they even kept the Disco Party out of office in the late 70s, though that was partly due to a mid-decade merger with the Funk Party. In the 80s and early 90s the Hiphop Nation was dominant, and now that Emperor's reign was coming to a close, many believed the Hiphop Nation would soon be back in the mansion.

It was almost two when Willie Bobo from the Hiphop Nation ran up to the turntables in a crispy clean white wifebeater, baggy sweatpants with the left leg rolled up to the knee, and a black Negritude U baseball cap clinging to the side of his head at an impossible angle — so obtuse that he was either employing glue or defying gravity. A thick gold chain hung halfway down his chest. At its end was a gold bust of his mother. He grabbed the microphone and said, "Yo, yo, Raggamuffin Projects in the house!" The candidates weren't supposed to speak directly to the audience during the debate, but no one could ever stop Willie Bobo. He was an unpredictable little being, now genius, then asinine, now violent, then tender, a grown man, but still a boy. Four b-boys in black Adidas suits and shelltoes with fat laces flipped into headspins and windmills as Willie spun the party back to the South Bronx and hiphop's founding moments.

It was a little shy of three when Cool Spreadlove's Princemobile roared up to the park, blaring "International Lover." Spreadlove waited as busty women poured out of the red Corvette as if from a circus clown car until one of them walked around the car's nose and opened his door for him. It was surprising that he had even made it. Spreadlove was never where he was supposed to be because he was cursed with charisma. Nothing was easier for him than making people love him. So all he did all day long was make love to people. He hadn't had a job in fifteen years. But he did have a bevy of Sugar Mamas who loved him so well that they supported him completely. Some even financed his dates with other women. He even had one of his women paying for his mayoral campaign. But you can be sure the little smidgen of juice clinging to the edge of his mustache as he strolled into the park wasn't hers.

Spreadlove stepped to the stage in a white floor-length fur-lined mink draped over his white Gucci suit with a white shirt and white leather shoes that shined like diamonds. He had long manicured nails and a freshly sliced basketball-size fro, so you knew he wasn't putting his hands on any records or any earphones over his doo. Instead, he had two fine mamas in short shorts and strappy stilettos running between the turntables, the crates, and his lips. Standing perfectly still, he whispered in their ears what to play, leading the party from an Al Green sermon about being tired of being alone to Prince saying you could smash up his ride — *well*, maybe *not* the ride — to P-Funk preaching about Chocolate City. That was always a Soul City favorite, but Spreadlove and his women got as much applause for their music as for their little show. Never let it be said folk don't like the theater.

Spreadlove had loved all sorts of women all around the world, but his kryptonite remained the blond, blue-eyed American white woman. He was transfixed by them, whether or not they were pretty. Just something about the sunshine in that hair made his mind all slushy. Emperor knew that if Spreadlove were mayor it'd be just a matter of time before John

Jiggaboo was invading Soul City. Ten years ago Jiggaboo had come to town looking to sell some shampoo. Emperor used the stuff himself and felt Jiggaboo Shampoo's malevolent tingle. He thought, There's something real funny about this shampoo, and promptly banned it from the Soul City market. Black people across the country fell in love with Jiggaboo Shampoo, but Emperor steadfastly refused to let it into Soul City. Emperor thought, Will Spreadlove continue my ban on Jiggaboo Shampoo? No. He'll probably invite Jiggaboo and his white women to come party in the mayor's mansion.

But Emperor wasn't too worried about Spreadlove. He knew there was no way Spreadlove could win, because Spreadlove never campaigned, because he was always having sex. What neither Emperor nor Spreadlove knew was that his women loved him so well that they campaigned for him behind his back, even when they knew he was off somewhere inside someone else. Spreadlove couldn't be bothered to look at the polls, but without even trying he was solidly in second place. *Anybody but him,* Emperor prayed.

4

S HE WAS lazing in back of the Biscuit Shop on her break. She was wearing Jimmy Choo heels with her Biscuit Shop uniform, smoking with postcoital aplomb. Her name tag said MAHOGANY. It was Saturday afternoon and on the city speakers Prince was droning on about a strange relationship.

She was being interviewed about her love life by a man from the *Soul City Inquirer,* paying as much attention to him as to her cigarette. She'd dumped yet another basketball player because even though he could fly, his superiority complex was too much for her. The whole city was buzzing.

She took a slow drag. "Flyin's gettin a girl nowhere with guys," she said drolly. "I hate men."

Cadillac was standing a few feet away, staring at his shoes, and eavesdropping.

The reporter asked her something about a prophecy, but Cadillac couldn't understand the question.

"I'm so sick of talking about that," she said, rolling her eyes.

With the trepidation of someone sticking his hand into the lion's cage, the reporter asked her about the rumors that Granmama secretly wants to die.

"I hate interviews," she said and dismissed him.

Cadillac's heart was careening around his chest. But with the hope of a man leaping with his eyes closed, he said, "Excuse me. I'm writing a book about Soul City and —"

"I get off in two hours," she said. She hated interviews, but she never turned them down. "Meet me right here." And that's how Cadillac Jackson met Mahogany Sunflower.

After work, in the parking lot behind the Biscuit Shop, she let him know that he was going to be buying lunch for her and her friend Precious Negro at a place in town that she'd choose. She told him she was driving before bothering to find out he didn't have a car. She was really bossy. Her car was a silver 1940 Mercedes convertible coupe with a white-rimmed fingertip-wide steering wheel and white leather seats. The ride was pristine except for the back corner of the driver's side, which was horribly crushed, the metal crinkling in like a hideous mouth. Mahogany turned the key and Billie Holiday's ancient, plaintive wail washed over them. The sound was so clear you could hear the uncried tears in Billie's throat. Mahogany and Precious sat there for a moment, listening so intently it seemed they were trying to go inside the music. He thought the car itself wasn't unlike Billie: rare, old, venerable, and once the world's finest. The crushed back corner spoke of Lady Day, too. The car had known tragedy and pain and was scarred, but had survived.

"I've never been in a Benz like this," Cadillac said.

"This is the fruit of lots of painful labor," Precious said. "This woman is the best baby-sitter in all of Soul City!" Mahogany had eight younger brothers and sisters, so everyone trusted her with their kids. "I'm her agent," Precious added. "For a Saturday night in the summer she gets one hundred dollars an hour."

"The important part of the story," Mahogany said as she turned onto Freedom Ave, "is that *this* is a Billiemobile." She'd gotten it at Groovy Lou's Loco Motives, the only place in the city that sold cars with a built-in jukebox that held all the music ever made by one genius. Your system would play nothing but the music of that one genius. That made your vehicle a sonic temple, a rolling emblem of you. "I had to have a Billiemobile," Mahogany said, "because she's a tortured goddess."

They cruised down Funky Boulevard and passed Groovy Lou's. Groovy Lou himself was outside arranging test-drives, which were really just listening sessions. He had a Ferrari Testarossa that his people had made into a Milesmobile, a Humvee converted into a Wu-Tangmobile, and a Cadillac from the 50s that was now a Jamesbrownmobile. There was a Beatlesmobile, a Gayemobile, a JayZmobile, a Marsalismobile, which played music by the whole family, and, his latest creation, a black stretch limousine with all the trimmings that was, of course, a Sinatramobile. The amount of care he put into his work was touching.

As they drove, Mahogany pointed out some of the town's landmarks. They saw the Gravy Shop, which boasted 186 varieties of gravy, 97 kinds of hot sauce, and Boozoo BBQ Brown's Patented Barbeque to Screw Mopping Sauce, which was known among aficionados as the hottest sauce in the world and, somehow, as an excellent sexual aid. They passed the Teddy Bear Repair Shop, U Drive-Thru Liquor Store, the Poetry Slam Café, and the roller-skating rink. They passed a Funkadelicmobile and a Monkmobile. They passed Dapper Dan's, where the legendary tailor would affix any high-fashion label to anything you wanted, from a hat to a suit to the interior of your car. He'd escaped to Soul City back in the 80s after the government ran him out of Harlem for trademark infringement. Now he was making Louis Vuitton leather suits, Gucci parkas, and Versace Toyotas and making some dead Euros do in-grave headspins. They passed Delicious Records, Bring the Noise Movie Theater, where yelling at the screen was encouraged, Soul Scissors, the twenty-four-hour hair salon, and Roscoe's House of Chicken N' Waffles. They passed a Biggiemobile and a beautiful Ellingtonmobile. Then they came to Lolita.

5

CADILLAC, MAHOGANY, and Precious walked into Lolita. Holden Caulfield lazily led them to a table and morosely tossed their menus onto it. "Bunch of phonies," he said and went back to the host's stand. He stared menacingly across the room at an oblivious Harry Potter, who was dutifully manning the cash register.

Lolita was a restaurant in Soul City's ritzy Honeypot Hill owned by a madman. No one knew his real name or where he'd come from. He'd arrived in Soul City thirty years ago calling himself Humbert Humbert. When they asked him where he'd come from, he said he'd recently escaped from a distressing little parody of a jail, but before that he'd been traveling around the country, sightseeing with his, uh, daughter. No one believed his story. They said, You can stay as long as you steer clear of our daughters.

Humbert opened a restaurant and forced his waiters and

waitresses to dress and act as though they were fictional characters. Sometimes this didn't work out so well. The waitresses playing Sleeping Beauty took the liberty of napping in the employee lounge as long as they liked. Whoever had to play the role of Gregor Samsa from *The Metamorphosis* was certain to call in sick every time. No one wanted to wear that giant beetle getup. The Cheshire Cat was always disappearing when you needed him, Cinderella kept losing her shoe, and Pinocchio was constantly lying about the specials. (He told the table beside them, "I highly recommend the rhinoceros testicles.") Professor Jack Gladney from *White Noise* spent all his time at the supermarket, Nancy Drew was always trying to figure every damn thing out, and of course the white waitresses were scared to death that Bigger Thomas would kill them. Not every character was a good fit. Lila Mae Watson from *The Intuitionist* applied to be elevator inspector, but despite her expertise Humbert judged her far too plain for Soul City and sent her packing. And don't even mention the insane little drummer boy Oskar Matzerath from *The Tin Drum,* crazy Dr. Charles Kinbote from *Pale Fire,* annoying Enid Lambert from *The Corrections,* snot-nosed Saleem Sinai from *Midnight's Children,* simpleton Jesse B. Semple, reluctantly slutty innocent Erendira (who was never left alone by her heartless grandmother), and that jealous wimp Gwyn Barry from *The Information.* They were all but impossible to deal with, as you can imagine. And no matter how much they docked her pay, Sarah Cynthia Sylvia Stout simply would not take the garbage out.

Humbert also had twenty-four large-screen televisions placed around the restaurant, tuned to the twenty-four-hour news stations. He liked to sit back and watch fictional characters coming to life and real people becoming stories and patrons getting intellectual vertigo. He'd wanted to name the place Mind Fuck, but he would've never gotten a liquor license.

Dolores Haze jumped down from Humbert's lap, nonchalantly floated over to the table, and took their order, standing just four-feet-ten in one sock, repeatedly glancing over her shoulder at Humbert, who was ogling her way too much. It seemed as though she was quietly hoping to escape. "This place gives me the creeps," Mahogany said, lighting up.

"So," Cadillac said, "how is it that flowers are able to come up through the concrete like that?"

"People always ask about the flowers," Mahogany said.

"It's difficult to explain," Precious said. "It has to do with the soil here being unpolluted. I mean, unpolluted spiritually."

"I don't follow."

"You don't have any way to organize the concept in your mind because it's so new to you," Precious said. "You're basically gonna have to learn an entire language before you can understand a word of it."

"That's why your little notepad's still blank," Mahogany said snidely.

Indeed, Soul City was refusing to be captured by his pen. He could see his book was going to take longer than he'd initially thought.

He asked if there was much crime in Soul City. They said no, very little. Well, OK, there was Hueynewton Payne, Precious's boyfriend, a seeming one-man crime wave, but he never committed his crimes *inside* Soul City. They explained that most of the Soulful looked out for their neighbor even when they didn't know their neighbor's name. For example, late one night on Mumbo Jumbo Boulevard, Jitterbug Johnson slipped and fell through a window, fell a story, and broke his arm. He landed in front of Spoonbread's, a twenty-four-hour French brasserie run by Spoonbread Sunraider, who had the seats arranged Parisian style — that is, facing toward the street so patrons could watch the Soul City sidewalk theater. Cool Breeze Blackmon and Audacity Brown were in the middle of a bottle of merlot when Jitterbug met the pavement. Cool Breeze jumped from his seat, snatched off the tablecloth without toppling his glass, and used it to apply a tourniquet to Jitterbug's bloody arm. Then Spoonbread used his red Rover to race Jitterbug over to the House of Big Mamas. There are no hospitals in Soul City because the House of Big Mamas is filled with mothers, grandmothers, and great-great-great-grandmothers — women experienced in every possible medical contingency. Yes, everyone in Soul City looked out for one another and that's why nothing ever happened.

That was the public story. In truth, though no one wanted to admit it, the person most critical to maintaining peace and morality in Soul City on a day-to-day basis was triple chinned Ubiquity Jones, master of the terribly timed gossip bomb.

The Soulful tried to keep their noses clean because they all feared Ubiquity Jones and her gossip bombs. Somehow, she always discovered your biggest secret and unveiled your dirtiest laundry in public at the most compromising moment possible. One day a few years back she discovered that Bootsy Jones, the official city gardener, had lost his mind one hot afternoon and enjoyed his eighteen-year-old apprentice, Sera Serendipity, while his wife, Sugarpie Jones, was home chasing after their three children. Well, that certainly wouldn't do. Ubiquity knew Sugarpie well enough to call her immediately and tell her in private, as a concerned friend would do, but Ubiquity was neither concerned nor a friend. A few months later, at the Day of Flight Festival, Ubiquity laid eyes on Sugarpie and sashayed over, her smile beaming as if a piece of the sun were caught in her teeth, her notorious triple chins bouncing as she honed in. She quietly stood near Sugarpie until a few other women noticed her standing near Sugarpie and, relieved she hadn't sashayed her chins over to them, surreptitiously planted themselves in her vicinity knowing what was about to be dropped.

"Aft-noon, *Mrs.* Jones," Ubiquity said in her fakest sweet voice.

A hello from Ubiquity caused most Soul City women to panic like a trapped rabbit, but Sugarpie refused to surrender her ladylike composure even though she knew a gossip bomb was coming. "Aft-noon, *Miss* Jones," she said stoically.

"Ain't it a shame . . ." Ubiquity said, letting her voice rise so the growing crowd could hear her end on a pregnant pause.

"What's that, girl?" Sugarpie said, cringing.

"Just the way your husband's been having little Sera for lunch lately!"

The assembled crowd gasped as one. Sugarpie was shocked silent. Ubiquity considered gasps and shocked silences to be her applause.

"Just tryin to help," she lied. "Now, how old is that little girl? Sixteen or fourteen?" Ubiquity knew exactly how old Sera was. "Cain't imagine how hard it must be knowin that while you're at home playin with your children, your man is out in the streets . . . playin with children."

Sugarpie, embarrassed in front of lifelong friends, crumbled into hysterical tears.

"Goddam you, Ubiquity!" she garbled. "How do you know?!"

"Oh, chile," she said, her smile beaming, her three chins bouncing. "Ubiquity is everywhere."

Sugarpie and Bootsy divorced within a week. They had been married fifteen years.

Now, if you didn't get your gossip from Ubiquity, you could get it from the *Soul City Inquirer*, whose twenty-seven men and women made it their business to know everyone else's business. The *Inquirer* had photographers and reporters swarming all over town, trying to figure out what everyone was doing, like a ghetto Big Brother. Thanks to them, all but the best-kept secrets flew through Soul City at Internet speed. Of course, the people at the *Soul City Inquirer* never shared any of their scoops with Ubiquity. They hated her. Everyone in

Soul City did. But somehow, despite all that rancor and all the manpower of the *Soul City Inquirer,* which occasionally rented a helicopter and flew above the city in search of gossip, Ubiquity Jones always had a monopoly on the best dish. They had no idea how she did it. Her secret was quite simple. Ubiquity Jones was a busybody and a mind reader.

She could read women's minds, but they were complicated places and took more effort. Men's minds were easy to read. All she had to do was look a man's way and she could rummage through his mind like a mental pickpocket. Anything salacious she found she saved in her gossip-bomb vault until the worst possible moment.

Just then a few of Lolita's twenty-four televisions flashed to a news report about the Soul City mayoral race. The *Soul City Defender*'s latest poll showed that with less than two days to go before the Soulful went to vote, the race remained a dead heat. "Looks like it's going to be a photo finish in the City of Sound!" the anchor said.

Dolores finally returned with their drinks, but as she placed the glasses on the table, Humbert stood less than an inch behind her, brushing up against her ass. She struggled to place the glasses without spilling.

"I fuckin hate this place," Mahogany said.

"You chose it," Precious said. She leaned in to Cadillac. "So, you ever do B?"

B was *bliss,* the newest drug. It was a brown syrupy liquid that you dropped into your ear. It made you limp and motionless but exponentialized your ability to hear. "It's like," Precious said, "you put your body in a coma and you just lay there, can't move, can't talk, but you hear amazingly." There was a tweaked gleam in her eyes and a romantic thrill in her voice. She might've been talking about a lover. "You can go *inside* the music," she drooled. "It's like LSD for your ears." Cadillac was reluctant.

Mahogany said it was a fun way to pass an afternoon sometimes. Precious announced that after they ate they'd go score and then go drop and that was that.

They were hungry and Dolores was nowhere to be found. "Good riddance," Mahogany said, taking a drag. "I never understood why people cared so much about the little raggedy slut."

Suddenly, the twenty-four televisions exploded into the self-important Breaking News song and dance. Then Hueynewton Payne's scarred face flashed on all twenty-four sets at once.

"Your boyfriend's on TV again," Mahogany teased.

"Oh shit," Precious said.

They watched Hueynewton emerge from inside a prison in The City. He was still in handcuffs, but his head was held high and his lips were pursed in a badass smile. Emperor Jones was by his side but shielded his face from the cameras. Hueynewton had been arrested in The City for the fifth time this year, this time charged with armed robbery and aggravated assault, after a daring solo daylight raid on a Kentucky Fried Chicken. He'd made off with a few thousand dollars from the store, seventeen wallets from the frightened customers waiting in line, and three buckets of chicken, which he calmly munched during a six-hour standoff with police. Thanks to some deft string pulling by Emperor Jones, just hours after the standoff ended the charges were dropped and Hueynewton walked right out of prison. When they took off the cuffs, Hueynewton turned to the media mob with the gleam of a crazy in his eyes and called out, "I ain't want the money or the chicken!" A reporter yelled, "Why'd you do it?" Hueynewton said, "I did it for sport!" Then he disappeared into Emperor's Satchmomobile and rode back to Soul City.

Hueynewton Payne was born in a tough section of Soul City called Niggatown and grew up on Fuck You Road. He was the great-grandson of Nat Turner, who rampaged through Virginia in 1831, chopping sixty white people into pieces, the bloodiest slave uprising of all time. The urge to be insurgent, to rebel, to revolt was not in the Payne blood — it *was* their blood. In the Payne house barely a conversation passed without a yell and not an hour went by without a fight because none of them ever had a feeling they felt wasn't worth fighting for. Hueynewton often found himself brawling with his parents over whether Soul City's mayor should play more hiphop, whether dinner should be chicken or fish, or who would hold the remote control. The passion they showed for causes small and smaller was topped only by their love for each other. Every fight concluded with a group hug that set everything right until the next fight, which was usually about ten minutes later. For them, fighting was a subset of love: an intense interaction that included high-pitched emotion, abundant physicality, and the opportunity to lose yourself. The Paynes found an ecstasy in confrontation, and though most others in Soul City couldn't understand the goings-on in their house, everyone knew the Paynes loved each other very much, despite copious evidence to the contrary.

But one night things got a little out of control. In the middle of dinner an argument over who would pass the peas to Hueynewton became a shouting match, then a wrestling match, then the parents Payne were grabbing each other's throats and squeezing so hard they choked off all oxygen to each other's brains, ending all conscious thought processing, and two people who normally knew where to stop went rumbling right past the line of no return. They went on squeezing increasingly harder for the better part of an hour, arm muscles bulging, heads turning red, steam shooting from hair follicles, neither willing to give an inch in the deadly blinking contest until, finally, they simultaneously choked the last bit of air out of each other. Both died at the exact same time. When someone arrived to remove the bodies, a crowbar was needed to wrest fingers from throats. Their orphaned son ran away to Whatevaworld in the Land Beyond the Speakers, a place no one in Soul City spoke of, where he lived for eight battle-filled years. If Soul City was the beautiful daughter, Whatevaworld was the horribly retarded son locked away in the closet all his life.

Years ago a small group of young Soul City boys decided

they couldn't stand bedtimes and vegetables any longer and sparked a revolution that led to an entire generation of Soul City boys running away to form their own society a few miles beyond the city limits. It didn't take long for them to discover that creating an orderly city is extremely difficult, and in short time their world turned into a nightmarish, ravaged Mad Maxian land. Yet every year a few Soul City boys run away to live there, away from grown men or any females at all. It's a land without intimacy, where survival is savored only by the fittest, fistfighting is constant, and hardcore hiphop booms through the speakers day and night. Hueynewton fit in perfectly.

His first month in Whatevaworld he beat down so many boys so fiercely that the leader ran away and Hueynewton assumed the throne. Leadership meant little in that rogue state, except that when there was food he always got some. Through the years Hueynewton had many long fights and adventures, and his warrior instincts were honed and sharpened until he was as fierce as a wild wolf. But as he grew older he missed the sweetness of soul music. He also realized that the reason there was no one older than twenty-one in Whatevaworld was because in a place run and populated by boys free to do whatever, whenever, it was impossible to last. Whatevaworld was an endless, parentless romp where bedtimes, vegetables, brushing teeth, and playing nice were unheard of. After years of improper nutrition, irregular rest, and seven or eight fistfights a day, either you were killed or your body gave out. So when Hueynewton was eighteen, one afternoon, while everyone

was asleep, he snuck out of Whatevaworld and went back to
Soul City. The day he came back he immediately became the
baddest man in town, Soul City's human junkyard dog, which,
by proxy, made him the only member of the Soul City Army.

It was fortunate that Hueynewton would never commit a
crime in Soul City because not only was he unstoppable but
there was no one around to try. Soul City hadn't had a town
jail in decades. There was no need. Most everyone was either
peaceful or scared of Hueynewton and Ubiquity. There was
even confusion over whether or not they still had a sheriff.
Doofus Honeywood had been appointed sheriff ninety-eight
years ago but had never been called upon to do anything.
When people asked him if he was still the sheriff, Honeywood
would guffaw and say, "If I am, I'm the last to know."

Because it was so rarely called upon, few realized that there
was indeed a crude justice system in place in Soul City. The
last time it was employed was in 1847, when Bottle-Eyed Billy
killed Gookie Dawkins.

Them two ex-slaves were in a bar, half-past drunk, when
some leftover rancor from their old plantation began to crop
up. The shouting got loud, the punches drew blood, then
Gookie broke a bottle in half. But that bottle ended up opening his own throat and he died. Nothing like that'd ever happened before and everyone wanted to make certain it never
happened again. So the elders convened to consider what the
punishment should be. Granmama was there and she said,
"The Good Book say an eye for an eye. What that mean to me

is: the other boy should fuckin die." So, a few days later, when it came time to bury Gookie, they put Bottle-Eyed Billy in, too. Thing is, he was still alive. He screamed as they threw the dirt on him, but he was tied to Gookie's coffin so tight he couldn't do nothing but scream. His wife tried to save him, but they held her back. Hours after all the dirt had been shoveled on that grave you could still hear him calling out from beneath the ground. After a while the yelling turned to whimpering. Then it just stopped. And no one's ever done much of anything in Soul City ever since.

They had no sheriff, but they did acknowledge that some outsiders weren't terribly enamored of Soul City for whatever reason, and someday they might need some sort of army to protect them. Few believed him, but Emperor Jones knew that even if the Devil had Soul City with its back to the ropes, Hueynewton would save them. The Soulful hated the way Hueynewton embarrassed them, made them a national laughingstock sometimes, but Emperor kept telling them that if they wanted Hueynewton as their army they had to tolerate him as their thug. So every time Hueynewton was arrested, Emperor Jones went running to save him. That was the cost of doing business with him.

They had no idea, however, that his latest crime would cost them all a lot more than they'd bargained for. The owner of that particular Kentucky Fried Chicken was the vile, billionaire shampoo tycoon John Jiggaboo. As Hueynewton walked out of jail a free man and Precious shielded her eyes, Jiggaboo was riding through The City in his limo, watching the TV in dropped-jaw shock. "I hate Soul City!" he screamed out, unleashing acid bile that burned a little hole in his stomach. The blonde at his side patted his back. He yelled, "They're just a bunch of nigger Muppets!"

Jiggaboo Shampoo was the bestselling Black hair product in history. In spite of itself. On every bottle was a picture of a jet-black boy wearing slave rags, his gigantic protruding lips about to bite into a slice of watermelon wider than his head while an overweight, handkerchiefed Aunt Jemima figure stood behind him, gleefully shampooing his pickaninny hair with a dialogue bubble over her head reading, "Jiggaboo make us happy to be nappy!" In the television commercials a pair of actors brought these garish images to life, and though the actors were physically and psychically repulsed by the work, they stayed because they were paid far, far above scale, getting hundreds of thousands of dollars a day. As they reluctantly said their lines, John Jiggaboo himself stood by saying, "Ain't it better gettin bookoo dollars to be a nigger on TV than gettin jack to be one in real life?"

A cartoon on the side of every bottle chronicled the misadventures of SuperNigger (penned by one Richard Franklin Lennox Thomas), a bumbling pseudo-superhero who always succeeded in screwing up whatever mission he set out to accomplish, tacitly proving the supremacy of the white superheroes. "Look, up in the sky!" the bottle's side says. "It's a crow! It's a bat! No, it's SuperNigger! Faster than a welfare recipient on check day! Able to leap the projects in a single bound! With X-ray vision that lets him see through everything but whitey!"

There were rumors that the shampoo that made your scalp tingle like no one's business also had a secret ingredient that made the shampoo addictive and seeped down into your brain and eroded your pride. This urban legend was repeated as often and given as much credibility as the stories that St. Odes malt liquor contained rat piss, Nixon Fried Chicken had an additive designed to sterilize Black men, the government once conducted a forty-year study on the effects of untreated syphilis on Black men in which the government withheld penicillin from the suffering men, and managers at Benny's were counseled by corporate to refuse to give Black children the free birthday meal the restaurant promised every child. (All of these, by the way, are true.)

But Jiggaboo Shampoo flew off the shelves because the product was actually astoundingly good on all types of Black hair, from Afros to dredlocks to Heaven-sent weaves. The streets called it "Kentucky Fried Chicken for your doo" because there was simply no shampoo that met curls, kinks, and naps of African descent and left them fuller, softer, and smoother. Jiggaboo even worked wonders on hair that was lyed, dyed, and laid to the side. The shampoo was a concoction that included aloe, beer, a dab of heroin, a touch of Kool-Aid, and a bizarre secret ingredient. It came in two types: for Good Hair and for Bad Hair.

Jiggaboo Shampoo was a success in spite of Jiggaboo himself, who made no bones about his contempt for Black people. He was born in Los Angeles, the spawn of a Black Hollywood superstar and a Black Hollywood prostitute. He was adopted by a pair of unemployed white actors who groomed him for the screen, and at age six he made the film that would define his life. In *Happy to Be Nappy* he played second banana to child star Nimrod Culkin, son of Macaulay Culkin, in a story about, well, who knows. The script was a mess, but basically, Culkin played cute and constantly rescued Jiggaboo, his semiretarded tap-dancing sidekick, a routine so grotesque even Hattie McDaniel turned in her grave. The script was actually written in the 1930s by a Ku Klux Klan grand dragon who shelved it because he felt it over the top. His great-granddaughter, a development executive at Fox, found it, tweaked it, and watched it make $100 million its first weekend. *Happy to Be Nappy II* and *III* did such boffo business that Jiggaboo never had to work again. Unfortunately, after years of playing that role, there wasn't enough money in the world for the amount of therapy needed to unscrew his twisted little head. By age twelve he was taking an antidepressive cocktail every morning and sniffing cocaine every night. His parents tried to reverse his growing self-loathing by getting him into the Hollywood branch of Jack & Jill, but "watching Nigroes trying to act white," he recalled in his autobiography, *The More I Like Flies*, "showed me that deep down Blacks just wanna be white."

Jiggaboo's personal unctuousness didn't significantly hurt

sales because Black hair is a deeply personal cultural crucible. Faced with a choice between OK shampoo backed by good politics and great shampoo backed by bad politics, thousands of Black folk opted for Jiggaboo Shampoo. Too bad they never knew Jiggaboo never used his own product.

Jiggaboo had never forgiven Soul City for banning him. Hueynewton robbing him and escaping punishment was the last straw. Jiggaboo was a man accustomed to getting whatever he wanted, and now he wanted revenge. He knew just what to do.

Cadillac, Mahogany, and Precious were beginning to wonder if their food would ever come. They looked around the restaurant for Dolores Haze, but it appeared she'd slipped away. They asked Holden if he'd seen her around. He said, "If you want to know the truth . . ." Then Humbert ran up, frantic. He cried out, "What has become of the light of my life?" He had no idea where she'd gone, and it was driving him even crazier than he'd already been. "I told her do not talk to strangers!" In the commotion Holden slipped away from the host's stand. He had something to get off his chest.

Stupid old Potter was always sitting there, acting like he was all earnest and humble or something. He acted so earnest he looked like he had a poker up his ass. But he was such a prostitute. Way more than D.B., and he lives in Hollywood. You never saw a bigger prostitute in all your life. Holden hated fistfights, but the bastard was always in the goddam movies, and if there's one thing Holden hated it was the movies. God, how he hated old Potter.

Holden walked across the room and socked Potter right in the jaw. The wizard collapsed in a heap on the ground, out cold. Holden stood over him, feeling good for a change. He said, "Goddam phony." In the commotion Cadillac noticed a young Black man in the corner trying to write, failing to come up with a word. The man looked strangely like him.

"Let's get outta here," Cadillac said. "This place is giving me the creeps."

"It's like living in a book," Mahogany said. "Who would wanna live in a book?"

In their haste to get out of Lolita, Cadillac, Mahogany, and Precious failed to notice Ubiquity Jones sitting in the corner all by herself, vacuuming up an entire turkey along with greens, grits, candied yams, black-eyed peas, stuffing, collards cooked with fatback, and a whole peach cobbler pie. She'd been reading Cadillac's mind since the three walked in and didn't think it at all proper for Chickadee Sunflower's oldest child and Dream Negro's only child to be running around Soul City doing drugs with a trifling reporter from The City who spent most of the meal envisioning himself and Mahogany in all sorts of filthy sexual positions. No, this would not do at all. She filed the news away and went back to her feast, waiting patiently for the moment she would drop her next gossip bomb.

6

———

BLISS WASN'T a polite little drug. It was some nasty shit. It took you on a journey into your subconscious, each drop warping your soul a little more. It was OK to dance with it once in a while, but you couldn't do bliss consistently. It was so new that no one was sure just what would happen to you. There were whispers that if you did a lot of it, your ear would fall off. No one had ever seen that happen, but bliss hadn't been around very long.

Precious knew they could usually find her dealer, Kilimanjaro, in the Raggamuffin Projects over in Niggatown. The Raggamuffin Projects were four tall, thin buildings that curved into one another at the top as if they were in the middle of a hug-a-long. It was originally intended to be a visual reminder of the power of teamwork or something, but the arrangement managed to block off all the sunlight, casting ominous shadows over everyone and everything inside the Raggamuffin

Projects. The buildings were so old that they were in the midst of crumbling, and without warning a brick could shake loose from the top of the hug-a-long and come flying down, as if the sky were falling, one brick at a time.

Precious led Mahogany and Cadillac quickly through a tricky maze of darkened project hallways. She navigated as as-suredly as a mouse through a maze that it has already learned. She knocked on a door and said, "It's me."

"You're back already?" Kilimanjaro said with an alarmed tone. If your dealer thinks you're buying too much, you have a drug problem. He knew bliss wasn't built for the constant use that Precious had fallen into. And he knew selling drugs to the daughter of the legendary Fulcrum Negro was danger-ous. He gave her a look like he wasn't sure if he should sell to her or not. Then he let her and her friends in. He was a drug dealer. He couldn't help himself.

Precious paid for two bottles and asked for credit on a third. Mahogany pulled her aside and said, "Your ear's gonna wither up like a leaf in the fall."

"That's bullshit," Precious said. But her ear had already be-gun to look a little more brown than normal.

They got back in the Billiemobile and eased down Free-dom Ave until they came to a green light and stopped. As they waited for the red light, Fulcrum Negro pulled up beside them in his Mahaliamobile. Precious waved to her father. Fulcrum wore long, flowing white robes. His dark, cracked, ancient skin was thick like burlap from Jesus's day and he seemed to

43

have angels floating behind him, singing hymns. Fulcrum was a founding member of Soul City and still a central figure in town. Emperor Jones was the mayor, the one the people voted for, but Fulcrum Negro was Da Mayor, the one the people listened to.

Mahogany and Fulcrum turned down their stereos. "I'm off to a meeting with Dizzy Gillespie," Fulcrum said. "I'll be back in a few days. Go by the store, your mother wants to talk to you. And what's wrong with your ear? It looks infected."

Wait, Cadillac thought, Dizzy Gillespie is dead.

When they turned onto Funky Boulevard, Cadillac saw the sign: FULCRUM NEGRO'S CERTIFIED AUTHENTIC NEGRIFIED ARTIFACTS. Beneath it was a smaller sign saying, DREAM NEGRO'S DESIRE OBLITERATING WEAVES. BY APPOINTMENT ONLY. Inside was a large, dusty, dimmed warehouse filled with glass cases. Cadillac walked around the room, and as he read the gold plaques beneath each case, he realized this was no ordinary warehouse. There was Charlie Parker's saxophone, Langston Hughes's notebook, Biggie Smalls's rhyme book, Arthur Ashe's racquets, Jacob Lawrence's brushes, Robert Johnson's guitar, Jackie Robinson's glove, Sugar Ray Robinson's gloves, Bill "Bojangles" Robinson's dancing shoes, Harriet Tubman's running shoes, Marcus Garvey's plumed officer's helmet, James Van Der Zee's camera, James Baldwin's typewriter, Malcolm X's AK-47, Huey P. Newton's leather jacket, Frederick Douglass's comb, Ralph Ellison's pen, Daddy Grace's throne, Stephen Biko's death shirt, Bob Marley's ganja pipe, and Richard Pryor's freebase pipe.

Fulcrum never sold any of the things he stocked. He knew all the things had a magic residue left over by the gods and goddesses who'd wielded them. Putting prices on such sacred nostalgia was unthinkable. Fulcrum had traveled long and hard to acquire the items and had gotten all of them directly from whoever had given them life. In every case he'd promised never to sell. And Fulcrum was a man who kept his word. That was essential for someone with friends in Heaven and Hell.

Dream Negro had never been to Heaven or Hell. She was just a hairdresser from Niggatown with a big-time husband, but she was essential to the well-being of Soul City. Her Desire Obliterating Weaves were the best weaves in the city. She told everyone, "Girl, my weaves be so good they bring you inner peace. After I finish with yo weave you won't want for nothing else in life!" She made so many women so happy on a daily basis that she was like a one-woman army beating back depression, low self-esteem, and poor self-image.

Cadillac and Mahogany were admiring Nat Turner's machete when Hueynewton rumbled up, his Tupacmobile audible long before he pulled into view. He slammed the door and strutted inside Fulcrum Negro's, his Tupacmobile idling outside, the music still blaring. Everyone knew he'd never once committed a crime in Soul City, but still, most people crossed the street when they saw Hueynewton coming. They were so ashamed that they wanted to spit when they saw him but so scared that they didn't dare swallow. He strutted into Fulcrum Negro's and called out, "Did y'all see me on TV?!" He was wearing a Soul City T-shirt and looking to have a few rough moments alone with Precious before he ran off to the big Negritude University football game. Soul City may have been disgusted by him, but he sure loved Soul City.

Outside there was a commotion. People were pouring from shops and stores to watch twenty men marching slowly up the street, chained together at the neck and ankles by thick rusty links. They were shirtless, shoeless, and wearing nothing but dirty burlap shorts, their skin sweaty and coarse, their faces weary and blank, their feet callused and cracked, their chains clinking in a garish rhythm, their backs crisscrossed by whiplashes. A fat man in a seersucker suit followed close behind holding a bullwhip. As the men trudged by, people cheered with the pride usually reserved for the military. Hueynewton ran outside and saluted them.

This, Mahogany told Cadillac, was the Slavery Experience, a yearlong odyssey that men volunteered for as a way of showing reverence for their slave ancestors. Neo-Slaves lived in shacks out in the fields at the edge of the city, picking cotton and getting whipped from dawn to dusk.

"I always wanted to do that," Hueynewton said.

"What?" Precious said, incredulous.

"Ever wonder if you're tough enough to have made it as a slave?"

"No," she snapped, her voice cold enough to slap the idea out of the air.

Then he and Precious rumbled back into Fulcrum's and found a closet. Five minutes later, clearly recharged, Hueynewton jumped in the Tupacmobile and roared off toward the game.

Cadillac suddenly found himself feeling guilty considering the bourgeois comforts of his world and the lifelong degradation of his slave ancestors. The privation and suffering you'd feel in the Slavery Experience could be like paying tribute to their ordeal. A sort of libation where you gave not your liquor but your pain, and you gave not a little but a lot. It could assuage the guilt, the slavery-survivor guilt he sometimes felt slithering through his spine. Then, Cadillac tried to imagine Mahogany as a slave, standing in the field in her Jimmy Choos, smoking with postcoital aplomb despite the heat. "No," she says to Massa while rolling her neck, "I will *not* be picking any fucking cotton."

7

MAHOGANY HAD a gigantic apartment in Honey-pot Hill with superhigh ceilings and a spectacular view of the Afro Pick. As soon as they arrived Precious jumped into preparing the B, but Cadillac stood at the living room window drinking in Soul City's great monument. "Ho hum," Mahogany said drolly as she breezed in from the bathroom. "I don't really see what's the big deal about Soul City anyway."

There were thousands of records stacked in milk crates that were layered to the ceiling, but no ladders anywhere. Cadillac imagined Mahogany flying to reach the records at the top. She had turntables, big speakers, a tower of old Soul Train DVDs, and a gigantic mirror.

As Mahogany sat on her furry white rug, Precious held a lighter to the bottom of a bottle. "It's better when it's hot," she said. He had a vision of basketball stars freebasing.

"What are we listening to?" Precious said.

"I wanna hear Satchmo," Mahogany said.

She pulled out a record and Precious placed the needle on the hallowed vinyl. Snap, crackle, and pop flowed from the speakers and Mahogany leaned her head sideways. Precious took the dropper from the bottle and placed three thick drops of brown bliss into the hole of her ear. Mahogany kept her head sideways for a moment, letting the liquid seep into her brain, then pulled her head straight up. In a moment her face turned zombie blank and a tear slipped from a motionless eye, meandered down her cheek, quivered at the edge of her chin, then plunged from her face. Precious eased Mahogany's limp body onto the rug as if she were a life-size doll. She lay there, seeming not to breathe.

Cadillac turned to Precious. "Is she alright?"

"Oh, she's better than alright," Precious said. "Your turn."

He turned his head sideways and felt the hot drops enter his ear and singe a path to his brain the way whiskey burns as it moves through your chest. Then his eyes glazed over and his body went soggy and he felt Precious lower him to the ground. He had no sense of anything and his vision was blurry. But he could hear Armstrong's magnificent triumphant croak. The sound became visual and he entered "(What Did I Do to Be So) Black and Blue" and found himself standing at the door of the cramped windowless room Armstrong was paint-ing with his voice. The light was dim, the mattress was spitting stuffing, rats were zipping in and out of view, and the wallpaper was bubbling and peeling as if the room were about to implode, and there was Armstrong, grinning the grin of a man who knows more than the eye can see, standing beside a record player saying, "C'mon, Pops, come check this out." He moved toward Armstrong and leaned down into the record player, his face inches from the needle, and suddenly he was inside the record, walking along the grooves of the LP, walking through peaks and valleys of black vinyl until he came to a man in garish blackface, his skin eight-ball black, his lips a white blob. The man said, "Niggas and flies, I do despise! The more I see niggas . . ." and took off his top hat as if to bow, passed it in front of his face, and was suddenly no longer in blackface at all, but handsome and dignified, with the soft, pleasing features of a model. He finished the song: "the more I love them." *Wait,* Cadillac tried to say, *doesn't it end: the more I like flies?* But now he was staring at a slave, his body ravaged, his soul crushed, his chains heavy, his face empty — Cadillac's own face. He reached out to touch himself and thought, *I have to help him, me,* then a thought came into his head, as if broadcast from somewhere else. *I'm fine.* He thought, *You're a slave!* The slave thought, *I'm a man.* Still, he felt the urge to save himself but knew not how, for now they were standing in the middle of Grand Central Station and there were whitefolks everywhere and they were walking around the slave, noticing him, not staring, but avoiding him, but they weren't walking around Cadillac. They were walking right through his body, not knocking him down, just moving through him as if he weren't even standing there. It didn't hurt his flesh, but it made him feel like his flesh meant nothing, like he was nothing, like he had no power over the space his own body occupied. He started to scream, but then he was trapped under a mountain of fat, listening to a bed creak like a large, wheezing, trapped mouse, and he was being squashed by a sandpapery walrus of a woman whose Black face he couldn't see. She shimmied her gigantic soaking body atop him, her skin smelling of burnt chicken grease as if she'd just come from the kitchen. And then she faced him. It was Aunt Jemima, naked except for her red kerchief, riding him with a face that got more furious by the second, thrusting hard and mean as if to injure him. There was murder in her eyes. She moved and a breast leaped toward him like a killer seal and whacked the side of his head, leaving her sweat on his face and the taste of greasy fried chicken in his mouth. She turned and said, "What's a matter, baby? Cain't ugly be beautiful?"

Cadillac wrenched his eyes open with his hands and found himself in a cold sweat. "I am not doing that again," he announced. He wouldn't tell them about the visions he'd had, but they could see the strange look in his eyes as he sat there twitching and trembling. Mahogany was embarrassed he'd had such a bad trip. Precious wanted to drop again.

8

A T HALF past seven on Sunday morning Cadillac felt
as though Saturday night still hadn't ended. His eyelids ignored his mind's commands and remained padlocked
shut. Soul City's unhurried air floated in through the windows
of his hotel room, and he felt he was changing, felt it just
barely, like the hairs on your arms standing up. But there was
no time for introspection. Revren Lil' Mo Love would be at
his pulpit in half an hour, and the sermons of the boy who
could preach like he was grown but hadn't read the Bible were
not to be missed. Cadillac shined his shoes with one hand while
holding an eye open manually, hoping maybe a little time in
church would cleanse his sins of the previous night and bless
his young book, which was so far going nowhere.

He ran down Freedom Ave, sweating into his suit, and at
five past eight slid into the most popular church in Soul City,
St. Pimp's House of Baptist Rapture, widely known as Baby

Love's because the pastor, ten-year-old Revren Maurice Love, was the son of the famous Right Revren Daddy Love, which is why everyone called him Revren Lil' Mo Love. The sermon was already under way.

". . . and I've gotta thank Mrs. Dawkins," the Revren said, standing in the pulpit atop two telephone books, "who was so nice as to take time out of her busy schedule to help me with my math homework on Monday night, and Mrs. Stickney, who left her home and came all the way over to the church to bring me a glass of milk Friday night as I was trying to write today's sermon." The first three rows were filled with grown women on the edge of their seats, fanning themselves furiously with fans that had Revren Lil' Mo Love's picture on them. They weren't burning up from the temperature inside the church but from the heat caused by staring intensely at Revren Lil' Mo Love, the most beautiful boy in all of Soul City.

He was just a wisp over four feet tall, with angelically gleaming skin, ceaselessly wet lips, and old-soul eyes wrapped in long, curled lashes that looked lapped by mascara. But the thing that dropped jaws lowest was his hair. Soul City called it the Sanctified Doo. And each Sunday after church people stood around deconstructing the messages he was sending them through his hair. The Revren was blessed with soft and silky chestnut brown curls so manageable that each Sunday he appeared in a different style: one week a gigantic fro, the next one cornrows, then it all blown out and straight, glistening halfway down his back. But no matter how it was shaped, the

Sanctified Doo seemed to gleam. This was possibly because
he washed the Sanctified Doo with nothing but holy water and
a shampoo and conditioner blessed by his mentor, the Revren
Hallelujah Jones. Today he'd passed the blessings on to his congregation with a glorious James Brown–style pompadour and
a little purple pinstripe three-piece suit.

With his beautiful Sanctified Doo, his Mighty Mouse ma-
chismo, and the untouchability his tender age granted, the
Revren was a magnet of such undeniable force that the sexual
tension between him and the women constantly around him
was as thick as chocolate cake. He used every bit of the power
his youth and beauty bestowed upon him to inveigle and fon-
dle Soul City's curvier citizens, and though it was true a few
had begged on their knees for carnal knowledge, he remained
the most hotly chased not-so-chaste virgin in the city. He paid
more attention to the females of his congregation than to the
quality of his sermons, but it really didn't matter. Whether
sermonizing or spanking a sinner, Revren Lil' Mo Love was a
natural. "You're just like your daddy," said devotees and span-
kees, and between the strange but soulful preaching and the
perpetual sexual tension in his church, it was absolutely true.

". . . and I'm so happy sweet Mrs. Lovejoy came to church
early this morning to grease my scalp and comb my hair so I'd
look presentable for y'all today," he preached. "And thank you
Miss Birdsong and Miss Delicate Chocolate. They spent the
last hour giving me the most wonderful manicure, pedicure,
and foot massage. Thank ya so much, ladies!"

The church applauded politely.

"Now, we in Soul City are privileged to consider God a friend of the family!" he preached.

"Thass, right, Revren!" someone yelled out.

"And when ya know God like we know God," he thundered, "ya get freed from a certain . . . *spiritual gravity!* Ya feel ya can fly even if ya cain't! Can I get an amen if ya feel your spirit's got wings because ya live in Soul City!"

"Hallelujah!"

"Is there anyone here-uh . . . !" he roared, "scared of going to Hell-uh!"

The congregation said as one, "NO!"

"Is there anyone here-uh uncertain of the grace-uh . . . !"

"Well!"

". . . and the perpetual watchful eye . . ."

"Bring it home!"

". . . of your friend and mine . . ."

"Come on with it, now!"

". . . the Lawd-uh!"

"No-uh!"

"I say, is there anyone here uncertain that they're going to Heaven?"

"NO!"

"Well good," he said, no longer thundering, just talking now. "Then let's have some fun."

"Hallelujah-uh!"

"Now, a few of you been sayin I need to refer a little more

to the Bible, and I'm gonna try. Once I finish it. You'll be happy to know I'm almost finished."

They applauded.

"So, today, as usual, we here to talk about our favorite savior . . . *Shiftless Rice!*"

"Tell it like it is, Revren! Tell it like it is!"

"Last week I told you the story of how Shiftless turned the slaves' water into wine . . . !"

"Thass right!"

". . . while turnin Massa's wine into water!"

"Hallelujah!"

"Well, this week we gon pick up where we left off, with Shiftless still on the Jerusalem, Lose-ee-anna, plantation of Massa Utterly Unctuous!"

"The belly of the beast!"

"One mo'nin Shiftless went into Massa Unctuous's massa bedroom to clean up and found Massa Unctuous jes then rising from a res-less sleep. Massa Unctuous say, 'Shiftless, my friend, I had the worst dream last night. A bonified nightmare.'

"Shiftless say: 'Let's hear it.'

"Massa Unctuous say, 'Well, I dreamed I was whippin this slave so hard my heart gave out and I died. But then St. Peter made a mistake and sent me to Nigger Heaven! There was garbage everywhere and it smelled bad. The houses was tore down, the fences was ripped up, the streets was muddy, and a bunch of raggedy Nigroes was sloshing around bein lazy and stupid. It was really scary!'

"Shiftless say, 'Know what, Massa Unctuous? I had a night-mare last night, too! I was out in the field pickin cotton when the sun got s'darn hot I jes keelt over and past away. That's when St. Peter sent me to White Heaven! The streets was lined with gold, the trees was filled with fruit, and the foun-tains was bubblin wit wine!'

"Massa Unctuous say, 'Shiftless, you said you had a night-mare. What's the scary part?'

"'Scary part's that I was in Heaven and there wasn't a soul in the place!'"

"Let 'em know, Revren! Let 'em know!"

"After a few years of Shiftless outwittin Massa Unctuous and performin the miracle of gittin out ah all kinds ah work, Massa Unctuous sold Shiftless to the cruelest massa in alla Mississippi: Bums A. Honkymothafucka!"

"Preeeeeach!"

"And even though it was Sunday mo'nin Massa Honky-mothafucka vowed he'd make Shiftless work! On Shiftless's first mo'nin Massa Honkymothafucka waddled out and say, 'Now, Shiftless, ya gone work t'day whether ya likes it or not! Ya gone start by pickin six load a cotton, cleanin the manure out the stables, and fillin the pig troughs, and if ya ain't finish alla that by noontime I'ma whip ya til ya wish ya was never born!'

"Shiftless say, 'Alright, Massa Honkymothafucka. But lemme asks ya somethin. Does ya like ta laugh?'

"Massa Honkymothafucka say, 'No, I don't! Ah ain't never laughed in alla my life.'

"'If I makes ya laugh right now, will ya let me out of cleanin the stables?'

"'Bwoy, ain't no slave in this world smart enough to make me laugh! For you to make me laugh would be a miracle. Tell ya little joke, and if I laugh I'll set ya free. When I don't, I'll whip ya but good, which is fuh sho all I been wantin to do all mo'nin!'

"'Well, it's late one afternoon on the Honky plantation and up in the big house lil' Ofay Honky's in the kitchen making a chocolate cake with the help of his mother, Honkie Honky. When Honkie turns around lil' Ofay dunks his whole face in the batter and whips around and say, 'Look, Mama! I'm Black!' Well, Honkie ain't one bit happy bout this. She grabs a broom from the closet and beats lil' Ofay's entire ass. Then she say, 'Go in the study and show your father what you've done!' He runs in the room and say, 'Look at me, Daddy! I'm Black!' Now, Mister Charley Honky don't find that so funny. He gets his bullwhip and whips lil' Ofay's ass summin good. Then he say, 'Now go out on the porch and show your grampa what you've done!' Ofay drags himself out on the porch and gets beat down a third time. When Ofay gets back to the kitchen Honkie say, 'I hope you've learned your lesson, young man!' Ofay say, 'Oh, I surely have. I been Black five minutes and already there's all these motherfuckin Honkys beatin my ass!'

"Well, Massa Honkymothafucka couldn't help but blurt out a big ol' laugh, and by noontime Shiftless was on his way to Canada!"

"Praise the Lawd!"

"But when Massa Unctuous heard Shiftless was free, he set the paterollers on him, and despite the deal with Massa Honky-mothafucka, Shiftless was soon back on Massa Unctuous's plantation, hungry for vengeance."

"Back in de belly of de beast!"

"One Sunday Massa Unctuous was in church and he got into it with another massa about which of them had the biggest, baddest slave. Them two bet a thousand dollars and agreed to meet that very afternoon to let they slaves battle it out! When Massa Unctuous, Missus Unctuous, and Shiftless was ridin on over to the other plantation, Massa Unctuous say, 'Now, Shiftless, there's a lot riding on this here fight. You do whatever you got to do to win.' Shiftless say, 'Awright, Massa Unctuous.' When they got there they saw the man Shiftless was to fight. He was twice as tall as Shiftless and had muscles upon muscles. He was chained to a tree, snortin and clawin the dirt like a hungry wild animal staring at fresh meat. Shiftless knew it would take a miracle to win that fight! So he walked over to Missus Unctuous and backhand slapped her across the face so hard that she fell to the ground and her skirt came up over her head exposin her bloomers!"

"Preach, Revren! PREACH!"

"When the manimal saw that, he ripped off his chain and sprinted into the fields!"

"Praise the Lawd-uh!"

"Shiftless was declared the winner, and one dumbfounded massa gave a stack of money to the other. Massa Unctuous ran over and say, 'Shiftless, how dare you touch my wife! When we get back to the plantation I'ma whip you til my arm fall off!' Shiftless say, 'Hold on one cotton-pickin minute, Massa Unctuous. You said I's to do anything possible to win the fight. Well, there wasn't no way for me to stop that man with my hands, so I had to use my mind.'

"'What you talkin bout, Shiftless?'

"'Massa, e'ry nigger know any nigger bad enough to slap a white woman is damn sho bad nuff *to murder a nigger!*'"

"Tell the truth, Revren! TELL IT ALL!"

"Well, Massa Unctuous ain't find that so funny. When they got back to the plantation Massa Unctuous tied Shiftless to a tree with his back in the sun and whipped him til he died!"

"Lawdy, Lawdy!"

"I say, he marched Shiftless right into the middle of Jerusalem, Louisiana, made him carry the whip himself, strapped him to a tree, and in front of a hundred folk he whipped him and whipped him and whipped him," he was yelling now, *"til the blood from Shiftless's back flew out onto Massa's face, and right up there on that there tree, Shiftless Rice, in the midst of a flock of body-snatchers . . . !"*

"Come with it now, Revren!"

". . . criminals of the flesh . . . !"

"Don't hold back one lil' bit!"

". . . in the middle of a gang of thieves, I tell you, Shiftless Rice was crucified!"

"PREEEACH!"

"But he was not forsaken!"

"No, he wan't!"

"*Ah say, our savior was NOT forsaken!*"

"Revren speaks the truth!"

"Oh, the dyin day was a good day for Shiftless Rice! Do ya know why?!"

"Tell us why, Revren!"

"I say, do ya know why?!"

"We's waitin on the answer!"

"*Cause then he ain't have to slave no mo!*"

"Hallelujah!"

"He immediately rose on up to Heaven, where he had a righteous warm welcome and was given a nice, big penthouse apartment on Amen Avenue in a neighborhood reserved for those who'd been in slavery, or suffered unjustly, or been wrongly persecuted. Mary Magdalene's mansion was just four doors down the road. Everyone on Amen Avenue liked Shiftless so well that after a few months in Heaven they nominated him to become an angel. God had taken an instant liking to Shiftless and accepted the nomination immediately. Shiftless was to become the first African-American angel ever! Everyone was pretty excited about it, specially Shiftless! So when St. Peter came down and laid them wings on Shiftless, he couldn't contain hisself. He started flyin all over the place, doin tricks and stunts and loop-de-loops, puttin more style into flyin than any angel ever had. And speed, whew! He flew so fast they couldn't hardly see whether he was comin or goin!

As with everythin, soon's we get our hands on it, we make it better."

"You know thass right!"

"Well, the white angels weren't so happy bout Shiftless's aesthetic innovations, especially one Pancho Pilot, and they complained to St. Peter."

"De whitefolks done did it again!"

"So St. Peter went down to Shiftless's apartment one night and talked to him about maybe slowin down a bit so's not to embarrass the other angels. Shiftless agreed, but soon as he got back in the air he couldn't keep his Blackness from showin and the next mo'nin he was out playin hide-and-go-seek with the clouds and tag with the comets! Well, Pancho and the other white angels went and complained agin! They wouldn't put up with this behavior at all. Said it wasn't dignified!"

"Tell it . . . !"

". . . wasn't sanctified!"

"Say it ain't so!"

"Wasn't angelic!"

"Betrayers!"

"Pancho and the white angels said if Shiftless wasn't removed as an angel they'd go on strike and there'd be not one miracle performed til they got their way! God could see they was serious, and as charming as Shiftless was, Heaven couldn't handle having all the angels on strike. So, on just his fifth day in Heaven, the Heaven Police grabbed Shiftless, took his wings, and escorted him to the edge of Heaven."

"Now that ain't right!"

"It'd been millenniums since anyone had been kicked out of Heaven, so most of the place gathered to say good-bye or good riddance. When they got to the back door of Heaven, St. Peter asked Shiftless if he had any last words.

"'Yeah,' he said. 'Life was a bitch and death's been just the same. I been in Heaven five days and already the mother-fuckin honkies are kickin my ass out.'"

"Praise the Lawd!"

"Shiftless considered makin a second comin, but he thought that after Heaven, Earth would be boring, and after slavery, Hell couldn't possibly be that bad, so he strolled on down to the Inferno to check out the scene. Shiftless discovered Hell was a world of plenty, where everything you could imagine was within arm's reach. He stayed a while. He ate juicy prime rib until he couldn't stand the sight of it. He drank fine wine until the smell turned his stomach. He was given a harem, and though it took a long time, eventually his taste for women began to wane. Slowly, everything he loved was being spoiled for him!"

"Lawdy, Lawdy!"

"Hell was much more tricky and pernicious than he'd realized. It wasn't any worse than slavery, but Shiftless hadn't been happy bein in slavery in the first place! So he started looking for the back door out of there when he glimpsed the most beautiful woman he'd ever seen! Her name was Madonna Satanas. The Devil's daughter!"

"Watch out now!"

"Shiftless went over and laid his game on her, and within minutes she was stuck on him. One night as they strolled through a river of fire, Shiftless said, 'Hey, baby, you know the way out of here? It's gettin kinda hot.'

"She said, 'Course I do.'

"'Well, you the finest thing I ever seen in my life. I could marry you right now and never look back! Let's you and me zip over to someplace a little cooler like St. Bart's, where we can jump the broom barefoot on the beach.'

"Madonna said, 'Shiftless Rice, are you proposin to me?'

"And Shiftless said, 'Yes, I am. I'd git down on one knee but I think I'd get burnt real bad.'

"They grabbed two of the Devil's favorite stallions, Hallowed Be Thy Name and Thy Kingdom Come, and raced toward the back door of Hell, way over in West Hell. But before they got there, the Devil noticed his beloved horses were missing and heard about his daughter's new man and raced off to catch them before they could reach the door!"

"Satan on ya tail!"

"Well, of course, he caught them, he's the Devil, and he tried to trick Shiftless and Madonna into sticking round, but they were too smart for that and before long a plain ol' fistfight broke out tween Shiftless and the Devil. Now ain't too many men can hold up their end in a donnybrook with the Devil! A scuffle with Satan . . . !"

"Tell it, Revren!"

". . . a melee with Mephistopheles . . . !"

"That's right!"

". . . a brouhaha with Beelzebub!"

"PREEEACH!"

"And there's damn few who would win! But we here talkin bout Shiftless Rice and Shiftless Rice ain't like other men. He was smart, fast, and highly motivated by the lifetime of top-shelf pussy riding on that fight!"

"Praise the pussy!"

"Plus, he was advised by Madonna that the Devil had a soft spot in the middle of his ribs on his left side, and a good punch there would leave him screamin like a hungry baby with a soakin diaper. Sure, she was betraying her father, but in her family they constantly betrayed each other. Shiftless punched the Devil in the spot and watched him curl up into a fetal ball. Shiftless took a stake from Madonna and drew a cross on the Devil's chest. Then the Devil had to bow to Shiftless. It was time to save some souls!"

"Praise the Lawd!"

"Shiftless and Madonna postponed their nuptials a few hours, passed out ice water, and installed air-conditioning units to make the bottomless pit a bit more bearable.

"'I'm only doin this,' Shiftless said, 'because you're gonna be my father-in-law and someday we're gonna wanna come back with some little ones, and if it's too hot we ain't comin. So don't mess with these here ACs because if you do, I'ma beat that ass again and turn this whole place into a giant icebox!' With that, the road was clear for Shiftless Rice's second coming. He and Madonna flew on out of Hell and over to St. Bart's in search of a broom they could jump and a hotel with outdoor showers!"

The service concluded with the organist, drummer, electric guitarist, and three-man horn section bursting into righteous riffs and the congregation clapping to the rhythm. The Revren yelled out, "May all our lives be filled with love, sex, and God! And where God will not provide, grant us the grace, courage, and cunning of Shiftless Rice so we might make it through! Amen!" The Revren stepped down off the phone books as though it pained his little body, thrust his arms out melodramatically, and moved through the aisles taking collection by allowing each member of the congregation to use a safety pin and stick a ten or a twenty to his suit. The ladies, of course, took their time, pinning on their currency like a delicate corsage and stealing a chance to touch his cheek or his hair or give him a quick kiss. As the Revren moved through the church he became a little strutting money tree. He stopped when he reached the church's back pew, and with the church thundering with claps and cheers and stomps and tears, the tiny Revren took the hand of a light-skinned, ancient man with paper-thin skin stretched so taut over his bones and muscles that you could see every vein and tributary and the blood pulsing through them. As the church roared, the man moved in slow motion from his seat to his feet and nodded with an augustness available only to the extraordinarily long-lived. "We love you, Shiftless!" someone yelled out.

9

AFTER CHURCH there was an impromptu reception in the parking lot. They all just had to chat a little before they got in their cars. Dream Negro, Precious's mom, helped Chickadee Sunflower, Mahogany's mom, navigate through the crowd. Chickadee was nine months pregnant. She knew it could come at any moment. She'd wondered if it would come during service. But Mama Sunflower wasn't about to miss a good sermon. Now, as the two walked slowly through the crowd, ladies were waving and wishing her well and the sun was out and the day was going so beautifully. But just then Ubiquity Jones was driving by in her Ninasimonemobile, listening, as usual, to her favorite song, "Sinnerman." She loved it when Nina sang, "Oh sinnerman, where you gon run to?" Ubiquity saw Mama Sunflower and Dream Negro together in a crowd and couldn't resist. She had somewhere to be, but she parked her Ninasimonemobile just to drop her gossip bomb.

Ubiquity rumbled into the parking lot wearing a hat with a brim so wide she cast a shadow over her entire giant body, as if she'd finally embraced her ominous place in their lives. Her triple chins jumped up and down as she bounced toward Chickadee and Dream, and it looked like the chins were rooting her on. As Ubiquity moved through the crowd women held their breath until she passed, then turned around to see where she was headed. They all feared the big, pregnant smile she always had before she was about to drop a particularly large gossip bomb. She was wearing that smile that day.

None of the gossips ever had anything to say about Mama Sunflower. She was beyond reproach, working hard at raising all those kids with a man who loved her to pieces. So no one expected Ubiquity to be heading toward her. But even if they'd known where she was headed, they couldn't have saved Mama Sunflower. Avoiding Ubiquity when she wanted to drop one of her bombs on you was as easy as avoiding Death when it's ready to take you. Ubiquity sashayed right up beside Chickadee and Dream, then hovered there a long moment so everyone would know who she was dropping a bomb on today. It was very rare to see Ubiquity sashay up to two women at once, and no one had ever known of Mama Sunflower or Dream Negro, both women from prominent Soul City families, being approached by the likes of Ubiquity. It appeared that history was about to take place in the parking lot of Baby Love's. Every single lady in the lot was listening.

"Mo-nin, ladies!" Ubiquity sang out.

Chickadee and Dream turned around and deadpanned, "Mo-nin?" Neither of them could believe that Ubiquity Jones had come for her.

Ubiquity took a deep dramatic breath to prepare herself. This was going to be good. "Ain't it a *shame . . . !*" she cried out, deeply pained for the fate of Soul City.

Dream trembled, but Mama Sunflower kept one brow tucked low, not ready to give Ubiquity her respect. "What? What!" Dream demanded nervously, as if she were asking to be shot sooner than later.

"That *both* of your daughters are running around town *doing drugs . . . !*"

The entire parking lot gasped as one.

". . . with a strange man . . ." She paused and looked around to make sure everyone was listening. *"From The City!"* She held back the news of his dirty mind, waiting to see the effect of these first two bombs.

Dream crumbled into tears.

Chickadee was embarrassed, but her chin remained high.

"Just tryin to help," Ubiquity lied.

"I will deal with *my* daughter on *my* own time," Chickadee said firmly. And then she cut her eyes at Ubiquity. The entire parking lot gasped again. No lady dared challenge Ubiquity.

Ubiquity took up Chickadee's stare and tried to read her mind but could find nothing with which to embarrass her further. She considered dropping the other bomb, but she could see that Chickadee was stubborn, a tough cookie, and Ubiquity thought she might need to sashay up to Chickadee another day because she certainly did not like the way Chickadee had challenged her. She liked to see women cry. Tears were her favorite form of applause, and Chickadee had not cried a bit. This would not do. She placed the other gossip bomb back in the vault and began waiting for the absolutely worst possible moment to drop it.

I'm gonna get you for this, Chickadee thought.

I heard that, Ubiquity thought.

10

MAHOGANY STILL felt guilty about Cadillac's bad trip, so late Sunday night she and Precious took him out dancing. In Soul City there are lots of places to go dancing any time of day or night, as is to be expected of a city with ten thousand DJs. Long after midnight the Funky Butt Dance Hall, the Soul Clap Café, and Cooley High were crammed. But that was never a problem at the Honky Tonk, so that's where they took him.

Mahogany was a local celebrity, and the *Soul City Inquirer* was always wondering who she was dating. If they snapped her picture in some nightclub alongside a guy from The City, all of Soul City would be talking. Just because Mahogany didn't like him didn't mean it wouldn't be scandalous. At the Honky Tonk they didn't have to worry. The Honky Tonk struggled to attract even a modest crowd because of its playlist: all white music, all the time. As they walked in, the Average White

Band was emphatically urging some white boy to play that funky music. "I fuckin hate this place," Mahogany said. She exhaled viciously. Someone slipped past and quietly handed Cadillac a card. They were recruiting for a secret mission to help bring the White Music Party up from the underground. Mahogany snatched the card out of his hand and tore it in half.

"You're out of control," Precious said.

"Look who's talking," Mahogany said. She tugged at her ear melodramatically.

Precious stormed off as Paul Simon limned a number of ways to leave your lover.

"Can you believe her?" Mahogany said.

He could. And he wanted to say so. Mahogany was a bitch. At first he'd excused it. He'd thought she was justified because she lived in Soul City. By now he wanted to say something to put her in her place, but Mick Jagger started crowing about the sweet taste of brown sugar, then Mahogany stood and the exquisite shape of her ass made him forget whatever it was he'd been thinking. She ordered him to dance with her. If she was a bitch, suddenly he was a puppy.

Most of the meager crowd leaped up to dance, too, and on the small dance floor they were pressed into each other, almost face-to-face. Then someone bumped them close and his lips made contact with hers for a single electric second. He was kissing her. She was not kissing him.

Mahogany's cellphone vibrated. It was her brother. She listened a moment, then yelled out. Heads turned. "My mom's having Epiphany!" she screamed.

Precious came running over. "The big moment's finally here!"

"What's that?" Cadillac said. They ignored him.

Mahogany had to get to her mother's side. Precious's excitement quickly dissipated and she calmly said she'd catch her later. Cadillac could see she was just waiting to go do more B. This was getting bad.

Mahogany ran to the Billiemobile. Despite her telling him no, Cadillac jumped in and refused to get out. He could see this was not something to be missed. His pen was in hand. Mahogany told him she couldn't take him with her. Her parents would be furious with her for bringing a boy from The City to their home. He told her if she left him with Precious the girl would try to get him high again. They zoomed off to the Sunflowers' house as Billie blessed the child that's got his own.

The Sunflowers lived in Honeypot Hill on Bluestone Road, number 123, in a tall, oval house that was shaped like a giant birdcage. Mahogany told Cadillac to stay in the car, then zipped into the house. She opened the door and for a moment he could hear a din, as if a tornado were inside the house. He listened to Billie for a moment, then crept from the car and peeked in through the mail slot.

There was no tornado inside, but if there had been it wouldn't have added to the raucous, riotous, clamorous, cacophonous scene of Mahogany's little sisters Magenta, Henna, Sepia, and the twins Pistachio and Cinnamon, and her little brothers Groove, Peasy, and King, leaping around the house as Chickadee screamed from her lungs and contorted her face and spilled birth juice all over, while Mahogany's dad, Sugar Bear, held Chickadee's hand and led her in Lamaze, and the midwife, Cocoa Serendipity, yelled at Chickadee to "Push!" as a head, two arms, and a belly slowly squeezed out of Chickadee's center: Mahogany's newest little brother, Epiphany. Sometime in the afternoon Sugar Bear had put on "A Love Supreme" in hopes of welcoming the boy with sounds of peace and love, but now all you could hear was a flurry of exalted saxophone notes flying around the room, scoring the moment's chaos.

The children were wilding, Sugar Bear was breathing, Cocoa was yelling, Chickadee was wilding, breathing, and yelling, and Epiphany — tiny, yellow, shivering, bald, wet Epiphany — was opening up his lungs and letting out a world-class glass-breaking scream that sliced the cacophony into silence. For one second. Then everybody went back to their madcap orgy of sound and fury and Mahogany zoomed in to join, crossing through the chaos of children to land at her mother's side as Chickadee and Epiphany struggled to separate themselves. Then Cadillac noticed Epiphany was more personally involved in the process of freeing himself from his mother than he'd known a newborn could be. With his bottom half still inside his mom, the little guy had opened his eyes and bent his arms down onto the stretched lips of Chickadee's vagina and was pushing himself up out of her, as if attempting to rescue himself from quicksand. He pushed, she squeezed, she breathed, he screamed and seemed more determined to get out with every passing moment, the centimeters separating him from freedom dwindling as his waist became visible and then his hips, Chickadee spitting him out as if she were creating him right then and there. When he succeeded in extricating one foot from her honeypot, Cocoa reached in and eased his other foot out. But then he wriggled away from her, grabbed his umbilical cord, and ripped it in two. "Grab him!" Chickadee yelled. But before anyone could, Epiphany stuck his flabby little arms out in front of his head like a swimmer, bent low, and zoomed up into the air. The boy was flying!

He flew directly toward the wall, banged into it, ricocheted off, and kept on flying, out of control and way too fast, zooming and bouncing off walls with the speed, spring, and elasticity of a racquetball, as his soft little penis flapped in the wind. Chickadee yelled, "SUGE!" and Sugar Bear took off into the air trying to grab little Epiphany like a loose rebound, but the kid was far too fast and flew too wild and whenever Sugar Bear was about to grab him, he bounced away. The chaos of children took off into the air and it looked like an aerial invasion and simultaneous counterattack, with children zooming through the air at every angle, colliding in midair and flying on. Epiphany was faster than everyone and happily scooted through everyone's grasp until finally Mahogany flew slowly into the air, watched the baby's path, bisected an angle, caught him, and calmed his restless soul in her arms. She floated down to her mother's side and the children began dancing in the air, doing flips and 360s and loop-de-loops, celebrating not so much the swelling of their ranks but the freedom the newest one allowed them. Chickadee took Epiphany in her arms and looked into his little brown eyes and told him she loved him, and he melted with the boundless ardor that's possible only with brand-new love.

Now Dad turned his attention to the chaos of his older children, and with just one look from him the anarchy ended, for though this was a happy home, it was also a dictatorship where the wishes of the czar and czarina were backed up by an army called The Belt and an elite force called A Switch From The Tree In The Backyard. Mom and Epiphany fell asleep and the house began to quiet and Cadillac walked back to the car dumbfounded, trying to make sense of the scene he'd witnessed: an entire family of normal-seeming wingless Black folk who could fly even at birth.

11

———

LATER THAT night Cadillac was in bed in his hotel room when he smelled something burning, the smell snaking in under the door. He got dressed and followed the smoke a few blocks to find a man standing in front of a burning Cadillac, flames leaping freely about the ride. He was shirtless, sweating, and playing guitar so intensely he seemed to be trying to cleanse himself. It was the JimiMan having a baptism.

JimiMan was born with the soul of Jimi Hendrix inside of him. He was a young guitar god who owned no shirts: all he ever wore were his leather pants and his guitar. A half-smoked, always-lit cigarette lived at the edge of his mouth. No one ever saw him touch it. He talked with it there, slept with it there, was even said to make love with that cigarette dangling there at the edge of his lips. He was the best guitar player in town, with an axe so cold he could freeze Soul City in its tracks. But he never knew if they were applauding him or the soul inside of him.

Earlier that day he was alone in his dark apartment, slumped on the floor beside a pile of marijuana as big as a newborn. He'd been awake for days on end attempting an exorcism by weed, hoping to smoke enough to forget who he was, but he'd smoked so much he just couldn't get high anymore. He'd spent an entire day soundproofing the walls of his place, then gluing another layer of soundproof foam onto the first one, then nailing up a third layer, only to discover that the sound he was trying to escape — the sound of Jimi talkin bout purple haze all in his brain — was coming from inside his head. But while Jimi was kissing the sky JimiMan was stuck on the ground, channeling someone else while longing for freedom. He loved Jimi. There was no one else in history he'd rather have had inside him, but it was his twenty-first birthday and what he really wanted was to be himself. But Jimi had consumed him so completely he didn't know who he was.

He jumped into his Jimimobile but turned off the stereo. In silence he drove to the corner of Freedom and Rhythm and began drenching his old friend with gasoline. The only thing tougher would've been drenching himself. He wanted to kill himself, but not to die. He wanted to be reborn. The car had defined him for the city, and for himself. Now it was completely soaked. He took one last drag, plucked the perpetually lit cigarette from his lips, and flicked it into the convertible. In

a blink flames erupted with a stunning roar and a wall of heat
sprung up. The car would die so that he could live.

The burning paint and leather fumed into an overwhelm-
ing odor and the smoke swirled as the flames danced upon his
ride, that flaming convertible, that Cadillac flambé, and then
he pulled his guitar into place and said something awful with
that axe. He began to play with the abandon of a man leaping
into a canyon with his eyes closed, unsure if he would live or
die, relaxed as if either fate was fine.

His fingers danced over the guitar with the thrill of touching a lover for the first time. He wasn't playing a song, wasn't
confining himself to a structure, he was just playing, impro-
vising, exploring his guitar and himself, getting to know them
both all over again. It was wild sounds full of questions and
fear, sounds in search of a song from a man in search of a self.
You could see the torment of discovery on his face as he
played alone in the night, his fingers filling the air with the
sound of his new life, his car aflame behind him, a meager curious audience in front of him. He was playing the autobiography of someone just being born. Playing not for applause,
but to find himself, to define himself to himself, and he
wouldn't have cared if they booed or cheered or walked away
indifferent because just getting to a place where he could ask
the question, *Who am I?* was victory enough for now. He still
didn't know the answer, but he was on his way and he'd play
til he found out.

12

———

O N MONDAY the Soulful marched off to vote. Cadillac needed a break. Soul City was amazing, but it surely was not Utopia. He went out by himself and accidentally found a little place called the Hug Shop. It was exactly what he needed. At the Hug Shop you could get a three-minute hug for $5, a five-minute hug for $10, or a deluxe ten-minute hugging experience for $25. Hug-a-longs, that is, to be hugged by two or more huggers at once, were also available.

The Hug Shop was the first in a planned nationwide chain. Its owner, Giveadamn Brown, saw professional hugging as the fast-food arm of the massage industry. Brown was as eager to please his customers as Ray Kroc was back when the sign in front of the first McDonald's said 1,000 SERVED. He'd run underground brothels and legitimate massage parlors, and his current venture delicately combined the two, hovering somewhere between the relaxation industry's legal and illegal branches. His huggers were not call girls, but they weren't trained masseurs, either. A sign in the window announced, HUGGER ON DUTY: ECSTASY JACKSON. He walked right in.

Ecstasy Jackson was dark chocolate with large pillowy breasts wrapped in a cashmere sweater. Hugging her would be like easing into a big brown curvy talking beanbag. Cadillac paid for a ten-minute hugging experience. She came from behind the counter and their bodies meshed. She put her arms around him, eased her breasts into him, tickled the back of his neck with her nails, let her perfume waft into his nose, squeezed his ass, and held him close and tight until he forgot where he ended and she began. When she finally let go of him, his body was jelly. He stumbled out promising himself he'd come back soon. But if he'd been a local he would've known why that was a bad idea. He would've known why a great hugger like Ecstasy was always single, why she was a sort of sexual quicksand.

He wobbled down the street until he regained his strength. Soon he found himself in front of the Museum of African-American Aesthetics (MoAAA) and stepped inside.

There was a new exhibit called "Black Is, Black Ain't. The Visual Vernacular, the Vernacular Visual." It featured art that, according to the brochure, "gives representations of Black culture through everyday objects, asking the viewer to look beyond the quotidian nature of the objects to see their cultural essentiality and thus artistic brilliance, which begs the questions: What makes up Black culture? What makes something Black? What does it mean to be Black?"

Video monitors were stationed everywhere. One showed a spry old man standing on a corner beneath a street lamp, but the film's true subject was his cigarette, his Newport, and the camera followed it from the moment it left the pack in his pocket on up to his mouth, then down by his belt as his fingers flipped and dipped and zipped — an anonymous, soundless magician holding court on the corner. There was a series of young men's lips, just large lips being licked in a bodacious, predatorily sexual way. In a separate room, all four episodes of *The Richard Pryor Show* ran back-to-back on a constant loop.

In a peculiar piece called *Whuppin* by Zeitgeist Jones — a leader of the Experientialism movement — the artist, a grown man, goes to his grandmother's house and asks her to whup him like she used to when he was little. At first she refuses. "Ya ain't done nuttin wrong, bwoy." He continues pestering her. "It would highlight the Black male's perpetual child status in America," he says. "And point out the sadomasochism inherent in the unrequitable love every boy feels for his first love, Mom, or, in my case, you, Grandma, a relationship that always ends in rejection for the boy because he can never attain the best girlfriend he'll ever know. And it would add me to the long tradition of masochistic performance art. In the early seventies an artist assembled an audience, gave a gun to a

friend, and had his friend shoot him in the arm." She cringes
at the thought. "Why don't you go run along now and make
another painting." He says, "But that's just it. Painting is no
longer sufficient to express the feelings I have about the Black
experience. Painting is flat and dead. The only true canvas that
exists is the body." She looks at him like he's insane. "Ah used
to tell yer daddy, *You just askin for a whuppin.* But ain't nobody ever really *asked* me fer a whuppin." He continues beg-
ging until finally she says, "Ah think all that art's gone to yer
head, bwoy. I wan't gunna whup ya, but now ya startin to git
on m'nerves askin and askin for a whuppin. So ah guess ah'll
whup ya fer gittin on m'nerves by askin a stupid question.
Now go out front and git a switch and if ya bring back one too
small, ah'ma go out there and find the biggest one ah can!"
We see him walk outside, pick a switch from a tree, pull down
his pants, and get whupped but good, for five, six minutes, until his thighs and backside are so red he can't even sit.

There were photo essays on the hi-top fade, a ten-foot bottle of Afro-Sheen, a sculpture of boys playing Cee-lo, twenty-
foot dominoes, video of Black Baptist sermons from around
the country, and a thirty-foot-tall *talk-to-the-hand* hand. There
was a wall of ornate gold medallions, from a gold Lazarus to
gold lion heads, gold grenades, and gold turntables, the Arabic
phrase "Allah U Akhbar," all sorts of Jesuses in various positions
and poses, and, the coup de grâce, an angel with exquisite wings
clutching an arrow being clung to for dear life by a short-

skirted angel who's being kicked in the eye by the first angel. It was clearly a battle between a good angel and a bad one, though a little difficult to say who was who.

On the top floor was a multimedia tribute to the Black male strut, the Afro, the ultratheatrical shoe shine, and the hand greeting, from hi-fives to lo-fives, including fist pounds, tight clasps, and finger snaps. And in the last room, the exhibit's finale, was the famous Steviewondermobile itself — a pristine money green 1983 Cadillac custom convertible with gold rims, neon green lights underneath, and a Harman Kardon sound system with sixteen speakers, wireless remote, thirty disc changer, and the clearest sound imaginable, a system that only played records by Stevie Wonder. This was the sexy beast that originally inspired the creation of the Museum of African-American Aesthetics.

The Steviewondermobile was previously owned by Huggy Bear Jackson, who'd donated it to the museum's permanent collection a few years back. That decision, based on art as much as hubris, proved incalculably ennobling for Huggy Bear. His benevolence turned him into a far greater hero than he'd been in the days when he'd cruised around Soul City, known as the man with the Steviewondermobile. Of course, unlike most people who make significant donations, Huggy Bear was neither rich nor smart. Donating the car meant he could enter the museum for free anytime he chose. It also meant he was without a car. But that's another story.

Outside the museum Cadillac sat on the lawn under a tree

and pulled out his empty notepad. He still needed a spark. One good first sentence, a sentence that would encapsulate Soul City, a sentence with just the right tone. Then the path of how to write about this place would become clear to him. With one true sentence that combined Soul City's beauty and its ugliness, the dam would break. But something Aunt Jemima had said had gotten stuck in his mind and was clogging up the gears. He'd tried to throw out the idea that ugly could somehow be beautiful, but the thought was so bizarre he couldn't stop examining it, the way boys are magnetized by dead cats on the side of the road. But now the bullshit detector in his mind had broken down and even the manual hand crank wouldn't work. If only the place had been a Utopia. That would've been easy to paint. It was easy to get the city's style and energy on a page. It was much harder to find the courage to be honest about both the beauty and the ugliness of Soul City. Writing, he felt, was like intellectual athletics, but when athletes conquered their fears and hit the big shot, the crowd roared. His courage would be taken as a betrayal, an airing of dirty laundry. No one roars for the courageous writer.

He sat there until the sun set but still couldn't write a word.

13

MOST IN Soul City do not know how to fly. Only those with flying parents have that gene. Those who have a gift get it the same way others get their height and hair color. Sometimes, when people of clashing gifts get married, their children end up with strange hybrids. But on those rare occasions when a gifted Soulful marries an outsider, their children never end up with a gift. That is why marrying the non-Soulful is so frowned upon in Soul City.

In the Sunflower family the ability to fly went back to their African ancestors from flying tribes that ate fruit from the tops of the trees, spoke with birds, and buried their dead in caves in the mountains. When Europeans arrived they chained down the flying people and carted them to America, only to find that the moment the chains came off, they escaped into the air.

Others in Soul City could read minds, or travel to Heaven and talk to God, or enjoy eternal life. In the late 1800s there

was a woman named Madame Dearly Beloved whose posterior produced a meaty, uncut diamond after sufficiently pas-
sionate lovemaking. The day she turned eighteen she married
Casanova Negro, Fulcrum's brother, had twenty-one kids, cut
a deal with DeBeers, and became Soul City's first multimil-
lionaire. Her philanthropy helped build the city.

Not everyone in Soul City had a gift, and some had a gift
they wished they could lose. For example, Ecstasy Jackson
could never get a date because everyone knew her love was
explosive. But sadder than the world of Ecstasy was the story
of a seventeen-year-old named Unicorn Johnson, who, right
around this time, tragically lost his life in Paris.

Now, how this poor boy from the streets of Soul City made
it to the legendary Ritz Paris on Place Vendôme is a long story
with something quite big in the middle of it. You see, Unicorn
had a Hope Diamond in his pants. That's right. Unicorn Johnson had the world's biggest dick.

Once upon a time, on a long, hot night in south central
Mississippi, smack-dab in the middle of slavery, a slave owner
named Cotton Fitzsimmons organized the world's first Cockfoster. Any idea that speaks so perfectly to so much of what is
felt by so many cannot be kept a secret long, so it took no time
at all for word of Fitzsimmons's invention to spread. Within
weeks the Cockfoster had become all the rage among upper-
class southern gambling gentlemen. Today, over a century
and a half after the end of de jure slavery, the Cockfoster per-
sists as part of an international underground subculture that's

swimming around the far edges of the modern zeitgeist like a prehistoric fish that's still alive because nature has not yet decided its day is done. The Cockfoster will run out of relevance the day the leisure class finds a more socially acceptable way of publicly interacting with naked Black male phalli. Ergo, never.

According to the sport's most respected historians, the Cockfoster hasn't changed a bit since Fitzsimmons's day. Around midnight, when people start getting around to real truths if they ever do, ten or so Black males are brought to a private room. They are paraded, fully clothed, in front of a gang of cigar-clutching white men who look them over, then place wagers on which of the Negroes will turn out to have the biggest dick.

Once all bets are cast a white woman comes out to dance for the boys, to make them hot. Then they pull down their pants so the blue bloods can see who's the biggest. No one ever thought of it as a homosexual experience. It was just a penile battle *royale*.

One long, hot afternoon not long before Unicorn's tragic death, a Cockfoster recruiter named Clarence Strider came rumbling into the outskirts of Soul City driving a Ford pickup filled with Negroes, lookin for jus one mo. Just round the hour the sun was bout to be gone Strider spied a six-foot-three, rail-thin, burnt-toast-black bwoy and screeched the Ford pickup filled with Negroes to a halt, nearly spilling some of his cargo.

"Wanna make five bucks, kid?"

Unicorn said sure and the journey began.

An hour before midnight on Friday, Jake's Gentlemen's Club in Ofay City began to fill up with white men wearing white double-breasted suits with gold pocket watches or seer-sucker suits with those little blue stripes, sucking Jack Daniel's or puffing Cubans, all of them senators, judges, tycoons: the lo-cal nobility. As the boys lined up backstage, nervousness pulsed through them like an electric current. Those Black boys were understandably afraid of getting naked in a roomful of massas. But when prodded by Strider, they hit the stage. The men turned wild and placed their bets. Very few went for string-beany Unicorn. And then out pranced young blond Miss Heidi Snowflake.

Heidi sashayed out, faced the boys, eased open her shirt, cut her eyes, licked her lips, winked, and teased until ten Black tongues were on the ground. Then she zipped offstage and the boys, screamed at by Strider standing in the wings, pulled down their pants and revealed themselves.

Before that moment Unicorn had never seen another man's penis, and, since he was a virgin, no one had ever seen his. He'd long wondered why the penises they had in the movies were always so small, but he'd really never thought much about his penis, outside of when he masturbated. He thought it was normal that when your dick got hard it sort of exploded out of your pants like a little tree growing up toward your face. He thought every man could push open doors, throw covers off the bed, or dial a phone with his dick. He ripped his pants down, having no idea he was no normal boy. But after a quick glance around, he realized he was more than four times as big as everyone else.

The monument between his legs was about three and a half feet long, with the circumference of a fist. It was a semi-arm. Everything about it was giant: His balls were like two apples, his hair made a big funky fro, his skin was so deeply wrinkled that the dick looked like a black baby shar-pei, and his hole was so large that a thumb could fit neatly inside of it, so large it seemed to be an eye, and men found themselves turning away when the eye looked at them.

The room fell into shocked silence, a deep, deafening anti-sound that allowed the sound of cricket chirping to invade the private club. Unicorn felt a hundred eyes on his dick, heard cigars hitting the floor, saw hats falling, jaws drooping, drool dropping. He smelled fear. The boys with him onstage backed away as if his monster had the power to hurt them by osmosis.

The other boys were hustled off the stage and Unicorn was escorted through the crowd by Heidi, who took his arm and whispered that Strider had said he wouldn't get his winner's $20 if he didn't leave it out. Unicorn never did get his $20, but he was introduced to the local nobility with his dick hanging hard in front of him, bursting from above his pants, which were open enough that the base of his dick could lie on them, creating the impression of a thick fire-hose blast of frozen black water pumped outward from a little fountain of fro. When they came to the 375-pound Senator B. Wary O'Wigglesworth, the Rubenesque representative stood to shake Unicorn's hand.

"That's a hell of a member there, bwoy!" O'Wigglesworth said, setting agreeing guffaws throughout the assembly.

"Thank ya, suh," he said shyly. He wasn't used to talking to white men with his dick hanging out.

"Where'd ya git it?" the corpulent lawmaker said, joking, and inferring, *Can I git one, too?* The caucus laughed harder.

"How'ya like to go to the regional championships?" O'Wigglesworth said. He turned to face the crowd. "Would he blow 'em away or what, boys!" A loud cheer rose up. He was a single, naked Black boy in a roomful of powerful whiteness. They could've tied him to the top of a tree right then and there and never felt the repercussions. How could he say no? And so, amid the cheering gentry and the Cheshire-cat-grinning roly-poly power broker, with his monstrous member hanging freely from his pants, Unicorn pushed past the extreme embarrassment of baring himself for a mob of men and agreed to debase himself yet another time.

Two Fridays later, a few minutes past midnight, Unicorn walked into a gentlemen's club and discovered his reputation was already there. The club was packed triple what it would normally have been for a Cockfoster. The cream of the region was already in the dressing room lotioning their jewels so they would glisten and shine under the lights. There was Kid Chocolate, Crazy Leg Hopkins, and, *from Nawlins,* Mordecai "Loch Ness" Moriale. This time, Unicorn noticed, no one was nervous. They strutted onstage, walking all cock-centered, staring menacingly at one another like arrogant champion sprinters before a race. They'd more than embraced their station and reveled in the small-time fame their bodies had bought them. The crowd screamed to bet, the white woman came out, the men pulled 'em down. Once again it was all Unicorn, a full foot longer than the next man, so intimidatingly elephantine that one contestant screamed like a bitch as he ran from the stage.

At the evening's end two men in slick suits came and told him of the national championships in The City. They offered to put him up at the new Trump Hotel and pay him a princely sum just to show up. He arrived two weeks before the event, and though the hotel was beautiful, the check never came, meaning he had not a dime of his own and couldn't afford to do anything but walk around. The new Trump quickly became a golden cage.

Yet the Cockfoster community was burning up over Unicorn, and suddenly the skinny boy from Soul City was giving an interview for the cover of *Nutcracker* magazine. They asked how it feels to lug this giant thing around with him all the time, what its name is, how he takes care of it, and what it would mean to him to be crowned the Cockfoster Champion of America. Unicorn had never had any deep feelings about his dick before his whole Cockfoster career started, had never named it, and couldn't have cared less about becoming the Cockfoster Champion of America. He'd just wanted to see The City. But he thought it'd be funny to muck around with the reporter. So he told *Nutcracker* it's quite a hardship to have a boa constrictor in your pants all the time, but I'm happy to bear the burden. Its name is Excalibur. I have a special drink called the Nigga Jigga, which I'll soon be bottling to sell, that I take the night before a Cockfoster to get me ready to get hard. And being the Cockfoster Champion of America would be the greatest achievement of my life!

But extreme fame in a secret community is a funny thing. He could walk the streets of The City by himself for hours, just wandering around. And then he'd bump into someone who knew him from the Cockfosters, a *Nutcracker* subscriber who invariably was a captain of industry for whom Unicorn was the new king in a secret royal family, and suddenly this captain of industry was in the middle of The City all but bowing to Unicorn right in front of his completely perplexed personal assistants. Unicorn moved from quotidian to sovereign and back in seconds. He started to wonder, *What am I doing?* But he was living at the Trump on someone else's dime in perhaps the most expensive stable in the world. When they gave him food he ate. When they put him onstage he shined.

Unicorn easily won the national championship, a full eight inches longer than Jim Browski from Brooklyn. As he pulled down the diamond-studded Versace jeans given to him for the night, his first serious girlfriend was hanging in the wings: Mellifluous Superfluous. They ran into the night together, danced on tables, sped in her BMW with the top down, talked about her modeling career, and kissed with the fury of people on a deadline. But, no matter how they tried, in bed they simply couldn't come together. Sweet Melly was six-foot-four in three-inch heels, extremely courageous and sexually ambitious, but she could take in so little of Unicorn's johnson that it was like sticking a finger in a keyhole. Ah, but Melly fellated his massiveness worshipfully, like the chocolate sculpture it was, and with her eyes always open to study the beast. Throughout their entire relationship, all three weeks of it, they were not able to keep the bed made, but despite that famous phallus, Unicorn remained carnally ignorant.

One morning the phone rang and someone with a French accent was talking about the international championships that were to be held in three weeks in the heart of Paris. He knew there'd be stiff competition from the reigning champ, India's legendary Piloo Armitraj, who they said could touch his nose with it, but all he cared about was seeing Paris. Melly insisted on going. She wasn't nearly enough woman for him and she didn't love all of him, but she couldn't live without his penis. She called it the steeple of the Church of the Miraculous Negro Phallus because that was where she kneeled down to pray every single day.

On the twenty-first and final day of their relationship, a Sunday, Unicorn left Melly in the Ritz and walked through Paris, taking it all in. The smell of croissants. The police siren, that slow, melodic two-tone whine. The goddesses who walked the streets trailing a wake of broken male necks with their long hair, balletic carriage, slit skirts, nylons, heels — fireballs with inch-long hairs that lay flat in their pits and nipples that popped out to greet you. Then somehow he stumbled into a museum where he saw the Hottentot Venus. There was the actual skeleton of the South African woman with the gargantuan posterior who was paraded throughout Europe in a cage in the 1700s like a curious wild beast or a circus sidefreak. And he could not help but think they were brother and sister. There was an implosion in his mind then, a reality attack, but it dawned on him slowly, washing down from the crown of his skull to his toenails, a dawning he felt as if he were ice cream being drenched in hot syrup. He walked back to his hotel room, dialed room service, and ordered a bottle of Jack Daniel's, four aspirins, and a large chef's chopping knife. The strange request from the giant star brought a manager and two Cockfoster promoters to his door. Unicorn, is everything alright? He said, "It's about to be." He drank a third of the Jack, gulped half the pills, then, in full view of the crowd, he dropped his pants, plopped his dick on the table, and with a single, furious motion chopped his massiveness into a nub. With the blood flowing as freely from his crotch as it had from van Gogh's ear, he ran from the room and down the streets, screaming like a madman, and dove headfirst into the Seine. The great river soaked up his blood, turned red for a day, then went back to its normal green. His body was swallowed by the river and never seen again. Hours after his death Melly was still in the hotel room, on the floor, mascara streaming down her face, hysterically praying at the Church of the Miraculous Negro Phallus.

14

———

EMPEROR JONES was dismayed. He and his aides had counted the ballots three times, and every time they'd gotten the same answer. It was Soul City election tradition that Wednesday at ten a.m. the old mayor's music would stop, the new mayor would be announced, and right then he would start DJing. But this Wednesday, ten a.m. came and went without a word from Emperor Jones, even though thousands were crowded on the lawn outside the mayor's mansion with collective bated breath. Inside the mansion, after many tense hours of vote counting, there was a clear margin of victory for one candidate, but Emperor Jones ordered that the ballots be recounted yet again. "This cannot be!" he yelled.

Soul City had made a grave mistake. Emperor shut the windows, locked the doors, and launched a fourth recount as the music stopped and Soul City was engulfed in silence. In order to let the people know he was still alive and working on an answer, he burned some paper, making white smoke emerge from his chimney. Each hour more smoke appeared, but for the Soulful the silence was like fingernails on a chalkboard. People began singing and clapping and playing homemade guitars, but it wasn't the same. The music that defined Soul City had stopped. The town shut down. Everyone came out from stores and restaurants, stopped doing laundry and playing basketball. A siren of silence had enveloped them in confusion. They had no idea what to do without some sort of music to underscore their lives. For five days the city stood in limbo, watching the hourly puffs of white smoke, waiting desperately for the killer silence to end, while Emperor Jones pulled the last hairs from his head as the seventh full recount yielded the same result as all the others, and he was forced to come out and announce the dreaded winner.

On Sunday at four p.m. the chimney produced black smoke. Emperor Jones put on his best suit and his fakest smile and opened the front doors wide. He tried to be happy, but it was just too hard. Soul City had truly disappointed him this time. The wrong choice had been made, the dunce of the group had won, and he knew that soon all of Soul City would be paying for it. "The next mayor of Soul City . . ." he said lifelessly, "is Cool Spreadlove."

Pandemonium ensued. The Soul Music masses leaped for joy as if they'd won the lottery. The Jazz people and the Hiphop Nation began citywide sulking. Spreadlove's campaign manager, Lovely Brown, ran up three flights of stairs, pulled him off of Sera Serendipity, and told him the good news. Spreadlove finished off Sera, then threw on his mink and hightailed it over to his new crib, the mayor's mansion in Honeypot Hill. As he walked up people were standing outside the mansion, drenched in silence, their eyes as vacant as drugless addicts. "We need some music, man," they said. "We're gonna die!"

Spreadlove looked them in the eyes and said, "I feel your pain."

He strolled inside and had one of his women pull a record from the stacks, put it on the turntable, and introduce the vinyl to the needle. After 102 hours of eerie quiet, the first record of his administration was on its way to the people. The Soulful smiled when they heard the snap, crackle, and pop of vinyl silence, and then, all over Soul City they heard Marvin Gaye and that honey-sweet, pimp-smooth falsetto, talkin bout let's get it on. "We gon be one city under a groove," Spreadlove told them, and he wasn't lying.

Spreadlove went directly for Soul City's libido, wanting the entire city to have as much sex as he did. All day and night he played records meant to induce sex and lust. Within a week the city had changed.

Spreadlove had the mansion's speakers put in the windows so the sound boomed out over the Great Lawn, and soon it was a place to picnic and party. The mansion became a twenty-four-hour house party, a carnival of free drugs and free sex with new panties constantly hanging from the chandeliers and the smell of sex oozing out onto the Great Lawn. An air of carnality gripped the city and the sound of bass-driven funk and soul was thumping day and night, and during the first two weeks of his administration, at any given moment you could open any window in Soul City and catch at least two people engaged in sexual congress. Spreadlove's soul and funk onslaught pushed the civic sexual tension to the limit and launched a citywide saturnalian fuckfest. In one corner of town Hueynewton and Precious were having sex so hard they fractured their pelvic bones. In a darkroom somewhere, Zeitgeist Jones, fully recovered from his whuppin by his grandmother, was suffering through a vicious spanking from slutty little Sera Serendipity. Over at Lolita innocent Erendira was making love for fifty pesos a turn with any man willing to wait in the hourslong line minded by her heartless grandmother. And down at the church, in Revren Lil' Mo Love's office, all standards were lost as the Revren was devoured and deflowered by Miss Birdsong, Mrs. Lovejoy, and Miss Delicate Chocolate.

Carnality was a mist slithering through the streets. Lust engulfed and blinded them like fog. No one knew whose bed he or she would be magnetized to at any moment. Late one night during this free-love frenzy, Cadillac was at the Biscuit Shop watching Mahogany spin.

In the three weeks since they'd met, they'd had no official dates because she refused to allow them to be called dates, but they'd gone to see *Coffy* at Bring the Noise Movie Theater, had had dinner at Roscoe's, and had gone late-night vinyl shopping at Delicious Records. But this certainly wasn't going anywhere. She didn't particularly like him. Besides, she was a Sunflower, and in her family you only dated others who could fly because only two flying parents could make a flying baby, and the Sunflowers had to keep the flying going. Mahogany was the oldest Sunflower of her generation, and for three hundred years the Big Mamas have said that if a firstborn Sunflower has a child who can't fly, that'll signal the beginning of the end of Soul City. Mahogany never believed the prophecy, but everyone else in town did and carefully watched her love life, groaning each time she dumped another flying guy. Everyone knew she would end up with a flyer, Sunflowers always did, but for the first time in years a Sunflower firstborn was having a hard time finding a flyer, and the town was getting nervous.

But that Friday night Mahogany wasn't thinking about all that. She wasn't thinking much at all. She was unspeakably horny. Nearly every man in Soul City would've dropped everything to go home with Mahogany Sunflower, but somehow Cadillac was in the right Biscuit Shop at the right time. When closing time came she grabbed him by the arm and took him home. Yes, all of this started because of what they call a lucky fuck. She knew he knew she could fly. She'd seen him looking that night at her mom's. So when they got into bed she climbed atop him, slipped her legs within his just so, and lifted up into the air, gliding in circles around her apartment like a child's toy plane. She had to be on top, that was just her style, so as they moved through the air he clutched tightly beneath her as if clinging to the underside of a sweaty, naked, curvy missile, orbiting her place ten feet above the floor while Prince seeped in through the windows and the cracks in the door. When she was about to come she doubled her speed and it got scary for him. He got nauseous watching the room spin around him upside down, but he wasn't complaining at all. She was riding the air while doing the same to him. He just had to try and hold on for dear life.

It didn't last long but was so amazing. Flying sex was incomparable. He had to do that again.

"We can't ever do that again," she said, as if she were afraid of herself. She was lying in bed, exhaling smoke, her heart pounding.

She'd loved the sex. His quick, rapid fear-filled thrusts had driven her over the edge in record time. But she was a Sunflower and a firstborn. They both knew it could and would go nowhere. So they did what young lovers often do. They did the least sensible thing possible.

They had flying sex again.

That's when she got pregnant.

15

———

GRANMAMA WAS bitter. She was 366 years old, but she'd long ago forgotten her age and banned all birthday parties, because she was tired of living. She'd seen it all and life had nothing new left to show her. She wanted to be in Heaven with her friends, but, as she put it, she was "cursed with eternal life." She knew she'd never see Heaven. Every morning she opened her eyes and grumbled, "This is fuckin bullshit."

Death has a certain smell that mortals can detect no more than they can hear a dog whistle, but Granmama and the twelve women who lived on T'ain't Road, in the mansion called the House of Big Mamas, could pick up Death's particularly putrid smell. With the head start their nose gave them they could run and hide or plan a trick and thus they all escaped Death over and again. Only way Death could even get near them was if their nose got stuffed up. That's why Death had decided long ago to leave them old girls be. Now, the Big Mamas couldn't avoid Disease, Pain, or Bad Fortune, so most of them were missing fingers or legs, were blind or deaf, were battling diabetes or cancer. But no matter how much the health of a Big Mama declined, she would not, could not, die. Thus, they were all well over 250 years old, Granmama probably the oldest, though Sweetness Serendipity was also past 350. Granmama couldn't tell her sisters in the House of Big Mamas that she wanted to die, because she was their leader and her death would crush them, would crush all of Soul City. But secretly, every night, she wished Death would come and see her while she slept.

On the morning of July 5, the Day of Flight, Granmama awoke pissed off about still being here. She dressed and made her way to Fulcrum's. The Day of Flight Festival would begin at noon and go on for twenty-four hours and the Biscuit Shop needed extra butter to deal with the surge in business. Fulcrum had gotten butter for her when he went to see Dizzy Gillespie.

Each of Granmama's biscuits took less than one-sixteenth of a teaspoon of butter, just a teeny dot, because the butter in Granmama's biscuits came from Heaven, brought back by Fulcrum. Fulcrum Negro could travel freely between Heaven and Hell and Here, a man with a multitemporal passport and an understanding of the very secret passageways linking the planes of existence. He called it transeternal traveling. Fulcrum made periodic trips to Heaven to see important souls and get things for his store and for friends in the city. He went to Hell far less often because the Devil always tried to trick him into staying. He went only for emergencies, like the night in 1980 when Richard Pryor was freebasing and set himself on fire. Pryor went to the hospital and died. After all the drugs, womanizing, and sin, Pryor went straight to Hell. But within an hour Fulcrum had negotiated a furlough that allowed Pryor a few more decades on Earth.

When Granmama got to Fulcrum's store he was standing out front waiting for her. His trip to Heaven had been fruitful. He'd brought back one of Dizzy's trumpets, five pounds of butter, some thread for the Teddy Bear Repair Shop (because sometimes they had to perform miracles), and, of course, hair for his wife so she could do more weaves. Course, Dream wouldn't be doing any weaves today. She was inside, in bed, under the covers, the sheets and pillows soaked with tears. Three weeks had passed, but she was still distraught over the embarrassment of Ubiquity's gossip bomb.

"Ubiquity's so impolite," Fulcrum said.

"She's a fuckin bitch," Granmama said. "How's Diz?"

"He's having a great time."

"Lucky fucker."

She took her butter and trembled over to the Biscuit Shop. As she walked a playful gust of wind that'd been born out over the ocean a few days earlier saw her alone on the deserted street and flew down to dance with her. As she angrily shooed the breeze away a germ floated into her immune system. By the time Granmama got to the Biscuit Shop her nose was a little stuffed and her supernatural sense of smell was clogged.

The Biscuit Shop was a beehive then, young women in dowdy uniforms racing around mixing flour, milk, baking powder, and the special butter, following Granmama's secret recipe. Mahogany was standing beside the turntables, yawning and smoking, slurping coffee, trying to get ready to spin for the early-morning crowds. In the commotion Granmama didn't even realize her nose was stuffed. But Death noticed. He was at a flood in Bangladesh collecting a bevy of souls, but he dropped them all, leaving behind five people slated for Heaven and eighteen scheduled for Hell, because after 366 years it was time to get Granmama. When he floated into the Biscuit Shop she didn't even notice. He laid back and prepared to finally do his job.

Now, Death is not the heartless guy that Hollywood makes him out to be. Listen to them and you'd think he was an agent of the Devil. This is not so. He takes people across and drops them wherever he's told. He doesn't have much discretion in the matter. He's basically a freelance soul courier. He doesn't even like Pain. (She's a *bitch!*) And he never understood why everyone loved his sister Life so damn much. She only had Earth to offer. After you saw him you might get to Heaven. So why'd he get such a bad rap? Sure, he seemed cruel at times, but just as often he was merciful. At the end of the day, he was just a working stiff.

Once, Death considered hiring a public relations firm to

change his image. He scheduled a meeting with the high-powered publicist Lizzie Benzman and floated into her office in The City right on time. As he moved through the office women ran shrieking and dove for cover. One woman called security, sobbing horribly, telling them Death was stalking the halls. Security left the building. Lizzie was in her office in a red power suit, talking rapidly into a hi-tech headset. She was a platinum-bottle blonde. Her hair made him think, *She's trying too hard.*

He sat down and calmly explained that he was looking to make a radical shift in his global image and was interested in hearing any ideas she had about getting people to think outside the box about Death. But she wasn't listening. She was trembling. She didn't want him as a client, but if she rejected him, would he kill her? If she accepted him as a client, would that mean she'd die at the end of the project? She fell to her knees and sobbed, "I don't wanna die! My daddy just bought me a *Mercedes!*"

He realized she wasn't listening. He was so pissed off, he took her across even though she wasn't supposed to go for another twenty-three and a half years. *Goddam phony,* he thought.

At the Biscuit Shop, Death watched Granmama in the kitchen, building balls of uncooked dough, hand molding them into shape, and feeding them to the oven, working elbow to elbow with girls a fraction of her age. But it was the Day of Flight and people kept coming back into her kitchen, interrupting her as she was trying to bake. Whether they knew her or not, the Soulful just wanted to come back and kiss Granmama. She was annoyed but she would let them kiss her and then she'd nod and make a quarter of a smile and say, "Now get the fuck outta my kitchen."

Even though Granmama wanted to die, Death could see this was a delicate situation. If she died something would die in all of Soul City. But if she didn't die today, she might never get her chance. He didn't *have* to take her. She wasn't on the list St. Peter had given him for today. Course, she would never be on St. Peter's list and that was why he'd come. He considered giving her a pass, but it could be another 366 years before he had this chance again, and there were others being born every minute and anyway, he was Death. He couldn't help himself. He looked into her soul and saw she desperately wanted to meet God. Then he floated over to touch her. He was just an inch away when she finally smelled him. Granmama turned around and faced Death and said, "It's about fuckin time."

She whispered, "Not in front of the girls," and they walked back to her office. She sat down on the couch and closed her eyes. He touched her as lightly as he could. Her 366-year-old heart slowed and then stopped.

16

MAHOGANY WENT back to Granmama's office to awaken her from a surprisingly long nap. No amount of shaking could stir her. Mahogany considered checking Granmama's heart, then banished the thought. Big Mamas don't die. But when more shaking and rubbing and coaxing failed to revive her, Mahogany began to wonder. She put her ear to Granmama's chest and heard nothing. She would've screamed but her mind rejected the idea that Granmama was dead like a bad transplant. When she finally dialed Fulcrum's cellphone, tears were pouring down her face, but she still couldn't believe it.

No one ever expected a Big Mama to die. You couldn't rely on the crutch of inconceivability, couldn't tell yourself the convenient platitudes we use to comfort ourselves in death, that everyone's time must come, that everyone's date is written somewhere. Death, the Soulful knew, visits everyone but the Big Mamas.

It took Fulcrum ten long minutes to pull a single coherent sentence from the tear-ravaged girl. When she finally choked out the words, Fulcrum was as shocked as she was. Then he ran off to Heaven to make sure Granmama was alright.

Meanwhile, the city was exploding with the Day of Flight Festival. People danced and drummed in the streets. There were step shows, stilt walkers so bad they were really stilt dancers, and the Shit-Talkin Clown with a punching bag for a nose, a role played with relish by Ganja Johnson, who bounced around getting in people's faces and on their nerves, talking shit about your nose, your clothes, and your mama. "Yo mama like a doorknob!" he'd call out. "Everybody done had a turn!" He embarrassed you publicly and pointedly, going on and on until you buried a fist in his big old honker. Then he moved away to pick on someone else.

Little girls collected wildflowers to place under their pillows that night in hopes of a dream that would reveal their future love. Most of the Big Mamas sat together under giant sunbrellas, healing disease for five dollars and broken hearts for ten. "Tomorrow, when the sun begins to set, make a moist warm towel," Big Mama Sweetness told Amber Sunshower, who was still devastated over her years-old breakup with Coltrane Jones. "Place inside it a sprinkling of baking powder, some bark from a favorite tree, and the dried leaves of a red rose. Take a long shower to cleanse yourself, then when you're dry, pour this holy water over your head. Let it flow over your body and do not wipe it off. Very important. Then hold the compress to your heart while you sip this John the Conqueror root. Then go to sleep. When you awake your ache will be gone, your mind will be clear, and your heart will be open to new love. But the healing will happen only if you believe. If there's an ounce of doubt inside you, it won't work. Faith is crucial to the healing. As with all things, if you believe it, it's yours."

There were competitions where the winner was decided by the size of the crowd's roars. First came the Neck Roll Contest, in which the ladies were judged on three criteria: velocity of the neck roll, width of the neck roll, and number of consecutive 360s they could pull off. In the final round Camilla Clothespony bested Sera Serendipity after an unbelievable ninety-six consecutive 360s, during which you could see only the whites of her eyes and her head orbiting her spine with such attitudinal force it seemed certain it would fly off. The Pimp Stroll champion was Revren Lil' Mo Love, who used his pint size and his daddy's rhythm to smooth-bop his way to the trophy. The contest for Sexiest Lip-Licker was over after Mojo Johnson took sixty seconds to moisten his top lip with his beautiful tongue, making women scream deafeningly and perspire profusely. And for the third year in a row, the Cocked Hat Contest was won by Willie Bobo, who strutted by the assembled crowd with his black Negritude U baseball cap at an angle so amazingly obtuse it would've made Sir Isaac Newton reconsider everything he'd ever thought about gravity.

All this was to celebrate the founding of Soul City. Many years ago Granmama, Fulcrum, and Sweetness Serendipity were slaves on a plantation that had a giant party every fourth of July. Every slave's stomach turned watching the whitefolks celebrate their mendaciously titled Independence Day. But in 1821 Granmama, Fulcrum, and Sweetness decided the insult was too great and that death was preferable to witnessing their fraudulent holiday even one more time. So after midnight, as the party roared on, they escaped on foot, running faster than they ever had. But a slave named Ignoramus Washington saw them getting away and screamed out. He ran after them, leading the search party, which chased them for miles. Granmama, Fulcrum, and Sweetness began to tire and their pace slowed. The three were just about to be caught, guaranteeing a grand lynching to help celebrate Independence Day, when suddenly a flock of Negroes emerged from the sky.

The flying Negroes were led by Moses Djembe, an ancestor of Mahogany Sunflower, the former chief of an African flying tribe and a recent runaway, or flyaway, himself. Earlier that day Moses had been herded from a slave ship to an auction block and sold for a princely sum. But when they tried to send him off with his new owner, he grabbed a hatchet, cut himself loose, then freed six others who could fly and led them into the air. As they coasted above the trees considering a return to Africa, they saw a band of runaways and flew down.

Hundreds of whitefolks saw Moses and six other Negroes fly down from the sky. They looked at these flying Negroes and tried to comprehend how inferior beings could have magical powers. There were implosions in their minds. Them whitefolks ran. But Moses didn't let Ignoramus escape. The entire group of runaways walked and flew together for weeks, all the while dragging him along. He kept yelling out for Massa in the same tone children use to call for their mommies. They finally found acres of secluded, uninhabited land, and though they didn't know what state they were in, they decided to make camp. Granmama said, "It don't matter none where we are. All that matters is the fuckin whitemare is over." They named their new home Soul City.

First thing they did was grab Ignoramus and hold him down. Fulcrum took a knife and opened the Judas's throat. As his blood seeped into the earth, Moses said, "This blood will purify this soil and allow us to live confined only by the boundaries of our dreams." They were free and so happy about it that they just sat still for an entire month, talking, laughing, and moving as little as possible. They'd been so hungry for freedom that their freedom was all the food they needed that first month. At the end of the month they began building a town, but they'd enjoyed a month of doing nothing so much that they decided they should do it every year. So they established July 5 as a holiday called the Day of Flight and designated the entire month a communal vacation. They called it the Month of Sundays.

17

FULCRUM NEGRO is one of the three living people who knows there's a portal into the path to Heaven located in Soul City. It's found inside the Lake of Roses, which, by some geological miracle, is over twenty times saltier than the ocean. When the sun is high the water takes on the color of a red rose. Because of the high salt content everyone floats in the lake, but Fulcrum alone can swim deep into it. Here he begins his journeys to Heaven.

Fulcrum's body can squeeze through the nodes that separate this plane and the others because he is a breatharian. Some people are vegetarians, some are fruitarians, and a rare few absorb all they need for sustenance from the air. The more solid food you eat — the more dead things you bring into your body — the more difficult it becomes to get your physical form through the nodes separating the planes known as Heaven and Hell and Here. Still, most breatharians cannot travel between the planes. Fulcrum was rare even among breatharians: he had never eaten anything in his entire life.

He dove in and stroked his way to the bottom of the lake, where he found a hole that he swam through, and soon the magical red of the Lake of Roses gave way to the ethereal blue of the River Jordan, which lies on the outskirts of the afterworld. Fulcrum swam for half a day until he came to the river's end. There he found the Desert of Doubt, a vast, windy wasteland that surrounds Heaven that you cross in minutes or millennia, depending on God's plan for you. This is where Death deposits souls bound for Heaven, but everyone doesn't make it all the way. The Desert of Doubt is a test every new soul has to face, a journey of spiritual endurance. There is no physical path out of the Desert of Doubt. God just wants to see you continue pushing forward despite the absence of any reason to have faith. With no clues, no roads, and no help, the weak of faith come to believe the journey is endless or pointless and give up and spend eternity there. But the faithful continue on even after there seems no reason to do so, and eventually God smiles on them and they discover Eternal Road and a plush chariot, a sweet-looking low-swinging chariot that's chauffeured by an angel who takes them straight into Heaven. And when they reach Heaven they find a gigantic flat field filled with happy, naked souls and nothing else. A beautiful, sunny, pastoral, open space — just a light sprinkling of grass, but no trees, no flowers, no hills. Heaven is a sort of spectacular nothingness, notable for what it is not.

Fulcrum, a veteran of The Path, usually needed five days to get to Heaven, but he was burning to see Granmama and completed the trip in under three days. Fulcrum stepped from the chariot and into the field. An angel pointed out Granmama. Her long life and deep faith had led God to speed her through The Path. She'd arrived just moments after her death and was now laughing with Dizzy Gillespie. When she saw Fulcrum she burst into tears.

"When I first got here, I thought, there's nothing here," she said. "This ain't no Promised Land. But as I walked through the field I realized I was naked and didn't want clothes. And then I realized I didn't want anything at all."

"There ain't nothin here," Dizzy said, "cuz there's no need. We're all happy with what we have. That's what you call peace."

"Have you met God?" Fulcrum said.

"Yes," Granmama said. "Wow."

"That's the only word that fits," Dizzy said.

"Anything like what you imagined She'd be?" Fulcrum said.

"Not at all."

"Was it a short talk?"

"Yeah, but it was right on time."

"Amen."

18

———

S EVEN DAYS after her death, as the sun began to rise, Granmama's slim coffin was wrapped in silk cloths of turquoise and magenta and carried slowly through the streets of Soul City by young men bookended by a brass band playing the bright jazz of a New Orleans funeral march. A teary muted throng of thousands lined the streets. Granmama had been a mother to Soul City and it was painful to know they would never again see her behind the counter at the Biscuit Shop or trembling down Freedom Ave. Yet Fulcrum's transeternal travels had made the Hereafter not an abstraction but a real place. Thanks to him, She was real to them, and when they spoke of Granmama being in a better place they didn't need faith to make themselves believe it. The Soulful had no more understanding of how the soul could continue on without the body than anyone. Yet to them, Heaven was a tangible place. The existential dread that grounds so many souls had no power in

Soul City because of their crystal certainty that some afterlife was assured them. Freed of that spiritual gravity, their souls lifted into the air of rare possibility like liberated balloons racing into the sky. As they said good-bye to Granmama's earthly form, they knew she was watching them. They knew they would hear from her through Fulcrum. And they all knew, as they knew the sun would rise tomorrow, that if they got to Heaven they would see her again.

The coffin reached the city cemetery and was laid beside its final resting place. The crowd that filled the cemetery was sad but smiling, tears falling down toward grins. Everyone was resolutely colorful: people wear bright colors to Soul City funerals — yellows, reds, blues, greens — colors of hope and life. The band played a few of Granmama's favorite songs. When they finished, Fulcrum came to the front and took a microphone.

"My friends, the moment I learned of Granmama's passing I went to Heaven to check on her," he said. "She's doing very well. She sends her love. She made the journey quickly, assumed a beautiful form, reunited with friends, and adapted well. I am very happy to say that Granmama has met Her." A sigh came from the crowd. "She is blessed and she is watching us right now. Let us celebrate her memory and let the knowledge that she's happy be a buoy to us. We miss her, but our sadness will be contagious to her unless we allow her happiness to be contagious to us."

The coffin was laid into the grave and each of the twelve living Big Mamas took a handful of dirt and tossed it onto her coffin. Thousands followed, tossing dirt into the void until it was filled. Then they all went to Paradise Park for a party. There was singing and dancing and chanting and laughing long into the night. It was a party not in her memory, but in celebration of her new place in the Soul City community. They had not lost someone. They had gained a friend in Heaven. She had not died. She had begun a new life.

19

_____

I T WAS early Sunday evening when Mama Sunflower sat down at the head of the table. As Sugar Bear carved the turkey, Mama cut her eyes at Mahogany. She'd been waiting all week to have a sit-down with her oldest. It was Wednesday in the rest of America, but in Soul City it was the Month of Sundays, so, once again, it was Sunday. It was actually the final Sunday of the Month of Sundays, which meant grand family gatherings throughout Soul City. Mama Sunflower had all ten of her children at her table. She also had a guest from The City. She didn't mind him so much. He was polite and well-spoken. But even though Mahogany was only two months along Mama Sunflower could see her oldest daughter was pregnant because moms can read minds, too. She was none too pleased. After dinner she and Mahogany would finally have that sit-down.

Across town the Revren Lil' Mo Love was fed like a king by

four women, two of whom forsook their own families to cook for him. Ubiquity was alone, at Lolita, reading all the men's minds, feasting just the same as she did every day. Precious, however, wasn't doing so good.

Her addiction had turned monstrous. She was twitching every few seconds now and hearing what people meant behind what they said. Her eyes had begun to droop and she constantly wore a hat to hide her ears, which were getting more brown and more brittle all the time. She was still seeing Hueynewton, but, like her ears, their relationship was getting sicker as time went on.

A few weeks earlier Fulcrum had discovered it was Kilimanjaro who was selling bliss to his daughter and told Hueynewton to throw him out of town. (The official message that Fulcrum gave Hueynewton to deliver was, Leave now or we'll convene the elders and decide whether or not to bury you alive.) As Hueynewton marched off to the Raggamuffin Projects, a distraught Precious called Mahogany.

"Are you afraid of what your father's gonna say?" Mahogany asked.

"No, I'm worried about where I'm gonna get my shit from now on!"

"You're really sick."

Mahogany didn't know the half of it. Shortly after Hueynewton expelled Kilimanjaro and confiscated his drugs, Precious found out she could get bliss from Hueynewton. She quickly ran out of money buying from him, so he started giving her bliss in exchange for sex, even though they were still going out. Sick. Mahogany had invited Precious to come for Month of Sundays dinner as a gesture of friendship, but she knew Precious would probably spend the night in some alley, dropping and listening to passing cars.

Mahogany didn't mind spending the day with Cadillac. He was cool. But the main reason she brought him to dinner is she thought it might somehow help her avoid the sit-down she felt coming on. It didn't.

Dinner went on for hours as the family argued and laughed, talking at the same time and telling stories on one another. Three-month-old Epiphany played with his food in his high chair, strapped in like an astronaut in his cockpit. He had so much energy he had to wear a seat belt in his crib at night.

Mama Sunflower and Mahogany didn't look at each other and didn't talk to each other and in this way came to realize that both of them knew that Mahogany was pregnant. Ten-year-old King Sunflower took advantage of the conversational void left by the two quietly steaming women and he talked on and on about his flying youth basketball tournament. He swore that this year Honeypot Hill would not lose to the bad boys from Niggatown. Mahogany promised to come watch him play in the tournament, but she would end up regretting going there for the same reason she already regretted coming home. "I hate being pregnant," she whispered to Cadillac.

After dinner Mama Sunflower and Mahogany had their sit-down. In Soul City there were other families who could fly, but somehow, long ago, the Sunflower daughters had come to be looked upon as a bellwether for the city's future. At the House of Big Mamas they'd long prophesied that if ever the firstborn of a firstborn Sunflower couldn't fly, then that would portend the end of Soul City.

Mahogany had heard the prophecy all her life and always dismissed it as a silly superstition. But nearly everyone in town believed.

"I don't wanna be the town talisman," Mahogany said sadly. But she already knew her baby wouldn't be able to fly.

20

———

WHEN HUEYNEWTON Payne rumbled into the town square that morning, for once they were happy to see him come. Hueynewton had finally decided to do the Slavery Experience, and today he was shipping out. A thousand Soulful were on hand and both the *Soul City Defender* and the *Inquirer* covered the event, which played out like a military send-off, with crowds waving the Soul City flag, nervous, tearful wives, and Hueynewton standing beside twenty-six men and three women as stoic and scared as young soldiers heading off to war.

They had volunteered for a year of dawn-to-dusk labor under the nose of a sadistic, whip-happy massa in a field on the edge of Soul City. For the next twelve months their lives would be exactly the same as a slave's. Exactly the same except that Neo-Slaves knew it would only last a year. All thirty knew they were marching into Hell, ready for an odyssey that would change them forever.

Most of the Soulful were glad Hueynewton would be off in the fields and not on their streets, but they were also impressed to see him show such reverence for his slave ancestors, like a good Soul City boy should. Hueynewton had just felt it would be a hardcore thing to do, like joining the Navy SEALs for fun. "I wanna see if I'm badass enough to have made it as a slave," he told a reporter from the *Defender*. Then someone clamped a thick, rusty chain around his wrists and he was linked to twenty-nine others. The massa yelled, and as Soul City cheered wildly, they trudged off into slavery.

Fulcrum called the mayor's mansion and said, "What'll we do if something comes up?" But Spreadlove had a shower running and twins from Honeypot Hill in there waiting for him. They were all gonna wash each other's hair yet again with the strangely addictive shampoo with the malevolent tingle that'd been sent to him before the election (but shortly after Hueynewton's KFC heist) by John Jiggaboo.

Across town pregnancy was making Mahogany bitchy, though it was difficult to see the difference between her prego bitchiness and her normal everyday bitchiness. She was complaining all the time, bossing Cadillac around, and missing her cigarettes terribly. But the morning sickness, afternoon sickness, and evening sickness weren't affecting her as much as people turning away when she walked down the street. Soul City had been waiting for her to become pregnant since she was born, expecting that she, like every other Sunflower firstborn before her, would get pregnant by a man who could fly. But now she was having a child that would never fly, and the Soulful were as scared as if she had a time bomb in her womb. Cadillac tried to help by running all her errands, rubbing her feet day and night, and allowing her to take her frustrations out on him. He wondered why she was so demanding when she was only three months along, but he kept this thought to himself.

Meanwhile, Jimmy Hustlemore, a photographer with the *Defender,* had his telephoto lens focused on the DJ booth in the mayor's mansion. Hustlemore, a beanpole-thin twenty-seven-year-old virgin, had heard the raucous rumors about what went on inside the mayor's mansion and could stand it no more. He had a case of sexual jaundice so advanced his brown eyes were turning green. Hustlemore blamed his pathetic pristineness on neo-Hefners like Spreadlove. He believed that sex, like money, was a zero-sum commodity, and for every erotic Rockefeller like Spreadlove, the Seducer in Chief, there had to be at least three sex-starved males missing out on their fair share of the action. Hustlemore watched Spreadlove spin records as a bevy of busty women sat around him giggling. Then, during a Barry White three-play, Spreadlove's eyes rolled back in his head and his jaw fell far open. Hustlemore quickly moved to another spot on the hill, zoomed in as tight as he could, and fortuitously snapped a single photo showing Spreadlove engaged in the sacred act of DJing for Soul City while receiving fellatio from an eighteen-year-old intern named Coochie Poontang.

The next day the photo ran on the front page of the *Defender*.

By nine a.m. the front door of the mansion was a swarming beehive of reporters. Spreadlove emerged from the mansion sometime after eleven a.m. wearing a scarlet robe. He said he loved music, loved Soul City, and had the utmost reverence for Soul City's music. And, oh yeah, that picture was doctored. "I did not," he announced, "have sexual relations with that woman while spinning!" But his pants were on fire then for two reasons: he'd lied and he'd been interrupted by the media mob in the midst of making whoopee. You could see the carnality in his eyes. You could smell the pussy juice on his lips. You could've scrambled an egg on his crotch.

The scandal sparked an investigation that dragged on for an entire month. It was revealed that his affair with Coochie had begun just a week after he took office, when she'd said hello by showing him her thong, then allowed him to play a game that involved hiding a Cohiba in her lower lips. They called this game Human Humidor or the Panatela and the Pudenda. Thirty other women came forward to say that they, too, had serviced him during that first month he serviced the city. Then, an aide with verbal diarrhea told a reporter that Spreadlove enjoyed about four or five women every day. The final report read like the Best of the Best of *Penthouse Forum*.

The people were enjoying Spreadlove's music, but concerns about his character and his lack of respect for the office of mayor reached fever pitch. He tried to stem the tide by introducing a new dance. No one liked it and he plunged even deeper into trouble. He'd been in office just over two months and already there was talk of impeachment. The *Defender* ran editorials demanding he resign. Spreadlove, backed into a political corner, told the *Defender* that constant sex was essential to the quality of his job performance. "The Soulful should take a lesson from the Parisians and take at least one sex break per day," he said. "Children need naps, adults need quickies!" Soul City didn't buy it. Spreadlove needed a big-time distraction to get people's thoughts off his penis, because as long as the whole city was on his penis, he couldn't put it wherever he wanted. His dick had put his neck in the guillotine, and he needed something to save them both.

Then John Jiggaboo called. He said Jiggaboo Shampoo was the number-one-selling shampoo in Harlem, East St. Louis, Detroit, Watts, and Chocolate City. Why wasn't it available in Soul City? He promised that launching Jiggaboo Shampoo in Soul City would revive Spreadlove's popularity.

Spreadlove said he loved Jiggaboo Shampoo so much he shampooed even when his hair wasn't dirty. He'd been using it obsessively for months and his hair looked incredible, but his brain was completely washed. One of his girls had told him some stupid rumor that if you used too much you'd turn into a bumbling boob like Stepin Fetchit, but he knew that couldn't be true.

Jiggaboo told him the rumor had been started by Johnson & Johnson as an attempt to kill his little Black-owned company. Besides, Jiggaboo said, how could a shampoo possibly do that? If Spreadlove had read Jiggaboo's autobiography, *The More I Like Flies*, he would've known Jiggaboo's personal motto. "A Black mind is an easy thing to waste."

21

———

J IGGABOO ARRIVED at the mayor's mansion the next day, bookended by a pair of underage blondes in flimsy dresses who reeked of sex so much that the three seemed to travel inside a smell-of-sex cloud. He was six-foot-four with a meticulously groomed, silky, shiny, young Michael Jackson–size Afro-of-life. Counting the fro, he was around six-foot-nine. It was a fro that froze you into dazed wonderment like the first sight of all the presents under the tree at Christmas, or your first look at an immaculate diamond. His nails were long and sculpted, his cane was carved and ivory, his cape was hellfire scarlet. Spreadlove and Jiggaboo had lunch, had each other's women, and then had a tour of Soul City. As they walked through the city Jiggaboo gave away a few bottles of his shampoo, but the Soulful who saw the bottles were too repulsed by the watermelon-munching pickaninny and the beaming Aunt Jemima on the front to do more than crinkle their brows and throw the bottle back at him. Then they headed over to Revren Lil' Mo's office. It was time for afternoon recess, when the Revren was allowed to entertain guests in the corner of the school yard.

As children ran and played behind them, Spreadlove said, "Revren, I'd like you to meet —"

"My God!" Jiggaboo cut him off. "Your hair is *spectacular!*" He circled behind the Revren to regard the Sanctified Doo from all sides.

"Thank you." The Revren beamed. "Yours, too." He said this nonchalantly, not wanting to show how impressed he really was. The Revren was used to having the best hair in the room no matter where he was, and having Jiggaboo in his face was like having a second rooster in the henhouse. *Is this guy a preacher?* the Revren thought. *If he's read the whole Bible, I'm in trouble.*

"But," Jiggaboo said, "I do notice a few split ends and a little less shine on the sides than the front." The Revren's heart raced. *Stay cool,* he thought, *stay cool.* Jiggaboo said, "I think I could help you look even better."

"What, what are you getting at?" the Revren said, defensively fluffing the Sanctified Doo.

"I am John Jiggaboo, maker of the world's greatest shampoo!" The Revren exhaled. "Nothing," Jiggaboo said, "has ever been made that makes love to Black hair like Jiggaboo Shampoo!"

He handed the Revren a bottle.

"What the?!" he said, seeing the grotesque pair on the front. "Is this a joke? Don't waste the Revren's time. I have other people to see."

"No, you don't understand," Spreadlove said. "This is some serious shampoo."

"I'll make you a deal, my little friend," Jiggaboo said. "Try my shampoo. If it doesn't leave your hair softer and silkier than it's ever been, I'll come to your church this Sunday and put ten thousand dollars cash in the collection plate. But if you like the shampoo, and I'm sure you will, promise me you'll let everyone know about it and I'll give you free shampoo for a year."

"Is it no tears like Johnson & Johnson?" the Revren said.

"I promise," Jiggaboo said.

After school Miss Delicate Chocolate drove the Revren home. He ran in the house, tossed his books aside, and jumped right into the shower. Miss Birdsong had scrubbed her hands and was ready to shampoo the Sanctified Doo. As she massaged Jiggaboo Shampoo into his scalp, the lather grew thick and the tingle was electric. He wanted to holler and stomp like he was in church. "I can feel the shampoo goin to war with the dirt and the naps!" he preached. "I can feel it workin and rumblin and rockin and rollin! This the Holy Rollers of shampoos!" When his hair was dry his doo had a glow. He'd never been more beautiful in all his life. He said, "I sure am *foin!*"

That Sunday in church everyone noticed the extraordinary

resplendence of the Sanctified Doo. To improve upon the Sanctified Doo was not thought possible, but the evidence was plain to see. The Revren spent his entire sermon on the miraculous new shampoo with the funny drawing on the front. When service ended they found Jiggaboo himself standing outside the church, selling shampoo for just $10 a bottle. After the Revren's endorsement no one cared about the drawing. Jiggaboo sold ten large crates in ten short minutes. Friends told two friends and they told two friends and so on and so on and in just a few weeks Jiggaboo Shampoo was in the shower rack of nearly every bathroom in Soul City. The Devil's plan had worked perfectly.

You see, years ago, before he entered the shampoo business, Jiggaboo met the Devil late one night in a seedy motel in Vegas and purchased the brain of Stepin Fetchit. Fetchit was a nigger. A Hollywood actor who took his stage name from a racehorse, he played the coonish, buffoonish, perpetually perplexed, impossibly asinine, and unrepentantly ignorant farmhand, stable boy, or slave with slow speech and bugged-out eyes in more than forty films, most made during the 1930s and 40s, all virtually Klan propaganda. The first Black actor to become a millionaire, Fetchit once had sixteen servants and twelve cars, including a pink Rolls-Royce, but by 1947 he was bankrupt. In the 60s he was a charity patient in a Chicago hospital. He died in 1985.

The Devil showed Jiggaboo how to clone the brain over and over, then grind the brains into pieces no bigger than a micron, and then put minute portions of the Fetchit mind into every bottle and thus into the brain of everyone who used Jiggaboo Shampoo. Of course, the bottles they made for the Soul City market were far, far more toxic than those for the rest of the country.

Now the Devil was inside the minds of the Soulful, with thousands of his tiny soldiers running amok, smashing mental windows. Now we would see the legendary Soul City self-esteem do battle with the pernicious microscopic enemies embedded in Jiggaboo Shampoo. The war for the soul of Soul City would be fought on scalps all over town. But, at the end of the day, don't it always come down to the hair?

22

J IGGABOO SHAMPOO hit hair with a vengeance, providing the distraction of premium hair care. It massaged and strengthened the hair while adding volume, body, and shine, and of course there was that malevolent tingle. But while it empowered the hair it unleashed a few malicious molecules from Fetchit's brain that moved like burglars sneaking into a bank. They slid into the brain through the holes of the hair follicles on a mission to get deep inside the gray matter, where they could cut down some of the ballyhooed Soul City pride.

The outer layers of the brain were easy to navigate for any cell small enough. But getting into the inner sanctum of a brain required ingenuity. Fetchit molecules swam through the blood-brain barrier and showed up at the gates of the gray matter dressed like an emergency cleanup crew. They tricked gray matter–guardian molecules into thinking they'd come to clean up a mess in the limbic lobe, where emotions are modulated.

Once they reached the limbic lobe they began to lick the axons with their toxic saliva. This often took lots of time because in a brain born and raised in Soul City the axons for pride were often quadruple normal size. But each time the Soulful shampooed there was a little more brain licking, or washing. After just a few weeks Jiggaboo could feel his shampoo working, could see people looking great while flying a little lower to the ground. Wash by wash the civic pride that electrified the city was draining away. Wash by wash Soul City was coming apart.

23

I T WAS a bonfire blaze stretching up into the night, the crackling so loud it sounded like cackling. Hundreds stood by in shock. Watching was so hard that only paralysis from the shock kept them watching. Their city was having a heart attack. A crucial little muscle powering the city was collapsing, bringing them all to their knees. Revren Lil' Mo Love's church was on fire. Revren Lil' Mo Love and his most ardent followers stood to the side, holding hands, praying silently. Some threw buckets of water, but it was a Band-Aid on a bullet wound. The fire ate all of Baby Love's and then went out. No one was hurt that night, but the fire ended up burning all of them. Long after the flames stopped, that fire was still burning away at Soul City.

The Soulful felt Baby Love's burning down was a death in the Soul City family, every bit as difficult to swallow as Granmama's passing. The wood of the landmark could be replaced, but it would never be the same, wouldn't explain who'd done this and why, wouldn't protect them from another attack. In the weeks following the burning no evidence emerged. The Soulful began quietly pointing fingers at one another. The trust and friendship that united them began to corrode.

The underground White Music Party became a suspect. It was rumored they had terrorist leanings, though they swore they were all about peace and love. Their leader, Oreo Feelgood, told reporters, "Can't we all just get along?" Then the spotlight turned to Jiggaboo. Despite his staggering shampoo, few in Soul City cared for him personally. But he had an airtight alibi: he'd been in the mayor's mansion, introducing Spreadlove to absinthe. This was not some clever trick. Jiggaboo had had nothing to do with the fire. At least not directly.

The broken-window theory holds that minor signs of civic decay are a gateway to serious crime. One broken window signals civic neglect. Leave it untended long enough and you end up with all sorts of nefariousness. Well, because of the shampoo, lots of windows had been broken inside lots of minds in Soul City. The air was thick with symbols of decay and no one had even noticed. First, a few people had danced off beat and no one said anything. Slowly, the proud peacock strut you saw everywhere became a lazy shuffle. A three-card monte hustler set up shop in the city square. In Honeypot Hill someone saw a rat. But Soul City was too anesthetized by the shampoo to do anything. Then came the fire.

Who done it? Was it the White Music Party? Jiggaboo? The

Devil? Maybe it was the bad karma cloud that'd descended on them and life was responding to the symbols in the air. No. It was Granmama. She was trying to get their attention.

Life's big moments are watched over and sometimes managed by God directly, but God is not Big Brother. She is not constantly surveying every little thing. We are not under twenty-four-hour divine surveillance. (We were a few centuries back, but nowadays human civilization is at the age, and maturity level, of teenagers and She can't be chasing after us every single moment anymore.) Thus, many Heavenly souls exercise their will over earthly moments beyond Her immediate concern. However, unlike God, with Her infinite power, souls sometimes find their abilities hard to control.

Granmama had seen the change that'd come over the city. It was a city in the midst of a quiet revolution. A devolution, really. They were slipping into blandness, which, for a place as dynamic as Soul City, was death. Heaven is teeming with Soul City fans who are always pulling supernatural strings on the city's behalf, but Granmama was so enthusiastic about saving her favorite city that the more experienced souls agreed to stand back and let her deal with the problem.

Before the fire Granmama had been talking with Moses about the burning bush. She thought perhaps a fire like that one would send Soul City a powerful message. But her aim was off and she missed her bushy target and hit the church instead. And more than that, the burning bush that Moses witnessed *did not consume its host*. Creating that sort of fire is exceedingly difficult. It took three experienced angels to put out Granmama's fire before it spread beyond Baby Love's. (Needless to say, She was not pleased.) Thus, with Baby Love's just a pile of ash, the city that'd been on the fence between the doldrums and the blues was shoved right into collective depression.

After the fire Soul City became a city of downturned eyes, where people were perpetually grouchy and stared off into space while meandering through the streets with a vague sense of purpose. They stopped saying hello as they passed. They stopped dancing through the day. They met the morning with a ho hum, as if they'd awoken in Albuquerque, or Cleveland, or even, God forbid, *Boston*. At first it was excused. It was said the city was in mourning. But two months later the city was still mourning as intensely as if the fire had happened yesterday. Their inner weeping simply would not turn into Life Must Go On. One night at the mansion, as Spreadlove and Jiggaboo sat drinking absinthe with their women, someone kicked out a power cord and the city's music stopped. It was an hour before anyone in Soul City noticed.

24

WHEN HUEYNEWTON looked across the field and saw gigantic Emperor Jones running slowly toward him, he wearily dropped his bag of cotton. His back was as tight as steel, his wrists ached from the weight of the chains, and his feet screamed from the miles of walking from cotton fields to rickety slave quarters. It'd been four days since his last whipping and he could still feel exactly where the lash had landed. He'd been a slave for four months and he knew he couldn't handle a lifetime in slavery. He would've killed somebody. The Slavery Experience had made him understand why Nat Turner had gone on his killing spree, but he sure didn't know where he'd gotten the energy.

Emperor explained that they needed John Jiggaboo thrown out of town immediately. Soul City had drunk the Kool-Aid of the new Black Jim Jones and the mayor had gleefully swallowed the most. Hueynewton tried to run, but he sludged his way into Soul City followed by a raggedy mob of slaves in dirty rags, hunched over or limping from aches and injuries. They had the spirit of crusaders storming in, but the look of zombies scraggling in.

Inside the city limits he could see they were in the midst of a meltdown. Drummers in the city's square were slouching idly against one another, their dusty drums silent. Teenage boys stood on street corners openly selling bliss. The flowers in the sidewalk were withering. The Vinylmobile had a flat. The scent of Heavenly biscuits was gone. Everyone stumbled through the city in a stupor as if suffering from mental leprosy, their minds falling apart as they moved along. Soul City was fading into dull sepia despite everyone's glowing dream hair.

The raggamuffin cabal reached the mayor's mansion and tried to break down the door, but their efforts amounted to little more than a firm push. After a few tries Hueynewton knocked. Two scantily clad blondes opened the door and asked if they were delivering the buffalo wings. It was late morning but the room was dimly lit and strewn with bottles and clothes and food and drugs and bodies conscious and unconscious. It was so messy it seemed a party had been going on for months on end, twisting time into a knot. The drapes were pulled tight and the air was stagnant and soupy and the clocks were broken. It seemed they'd been so wanton and feckless so long that even this had begun to bore, and complete spiritual inertia had set up shop. Hueynewton climbed up to the third floor, opened a door, and found Spreadlove lying on the floor, sucking on an opium pipe, his eyelids below half-mast, being massaged by a pair of nearly naked blondes. "Boo, is that you?" the mayor gargled. "I need some more shampoo."

Hueynewton found the Black Jim Jones in the DJ booth, behind the turntables. He had a Barry Manilow record in his hand. Hueynewton shuddered at the thought of his city hearing that ultrawhite man warbling about the goddam Copacabana. At a time of spiritual vulnerability like this, a moment of Manilow could ruin Soul City forever. Hueynewton tried to lunge at Jiggaboo, but he sort of lamely jumped up and chest bumped him into the wall, knocking the turntables to the floor so the sound of the needle screeching across a record ripped through the city. Jiggaboo wriggled free from Hueynewton's weak bear hug and swung at him, but missed. He steadied himself, then swung and missed again, losing his balance and falling to the floor. He was really high. They were men of unbreakable will, but neither was in any condition to fight. Jiggaboo had the Devil instructing him telepathically while Granmama urged Hueynewton on. It was a miniwar over the future of Soul City, played out in front of Heaven and Hell. Yet the fighting was pathetic.

Jiggaboo threw a turntable at Hueynewton. He aimed for his head but hit him in the shin. Hueynewton fell back from the pain, hit his head on the wall, and fell out cold. The Devil was embarrassed for them both. Jiggaboo took a moment to catch his breath, then grabbed a bottle of shampoo from the floor. He poured half the bottle on Hueynewton's hair and began furiously working the shampoo into his head, scrubbing as if Hueynewton was his dirt-caked son, until his hands were invisible beneath malevolent lather. He was trying to push the Fetchitness into Hueynewton's scalp with his fingers and hasten the zombification of Soul City's last hope. But Granmama would not let her boy lose. She yelled into the ear in his mind, "Git the *fuck* up!"

Hueynewton came to and felt the wild tingling on his scalp. He pushed Jiggaboo off of him and said, "What is wrong with you?" Hueynewton would've attacked him, but he was spent.

Jiggaboo struggled to balance himself like a toddler. "I can't stand you Soul City niggers!" he said, spitting while he spewed. "You're just a bunch of dancing, boppity boho Black nigger Muppets with funny names and stupid cars." He wiped his mouth with his sleeve. "You flying Negroes make me sick!"

Hueynewton took hold of the wobbling Jiggaboo as if to help him stand. He said, "Nobody calls our names funny." Then he pushed him toward the window. It was actually an attempt to throw him out the window, but Jiggaboo's head hit the top of the windowsill and he fell on the floor and lay there drooling. Now the Devil was really embarrassed. Hueynewton pulled Jiggaboo off the floor and lamely dumped him out the window. Jiggaboo fell two stories and landed on the windshield of Spreadlove's Princemobile. He went straight through the glass and broke his neck on the steering wheel. Death was right there to scoop him up. "I know where I'm goin,'" Jiggaboo grumbled as Death led him away.

Hueynewton stumbled out of the mansion and fell asleep on the Great Lawn. He was bloodied and bruised, but he had great-looking hair.

When Spreadlove sobered up he had a meeting with Fulcrum.

"If you resign now," Fulcrum said, "you can go on living in Soul City. If you refuse to resign you'll have a hearing where you'll be judged by the city's elders and you'll be able to argue your side. We might agree to let you continue being mayor. Probably not, but you never know. We may exile you from the city forever. Or we could opt to bury you alive in the cemetery. Probably not. But you never know."

Spreadlove's hasty resignation was accepted. He was mayor for all of six months. Fulcrum picked Emperor Jones to finish out Spreadlove's term. He assumed that Jiggaboo had burned down the church, but they never found any proof. He always thought it very curious that even though Granmama had been looking down from Heaven when it happened, she had no idea who'd done it.

The next night there was a Jiggaboo Shampoo bonfire in Paradise Park. Most threw in their bottles happily, but a few were reluctant to give up theirs. Fulcrum asked Hueynewton to help them change their minds. He was persuasive, as usual. It was a glorious night. The drummers returned to drumming, the sidewalk flowers began blooming, and Ecstasy Jackson prowled the park hugging everyone for free. She was sexy and offering her number to all the men, willing to sleep with any-one, but nobody would go to bed with her. She was theoreti-cally Soul City's easiest girl, but she was a virgin because the whole town knew her family's secret. Finally, Hueynewton was brought to the front of the crowd and hailed as the man who beat down an agent of the Devil and saved Soul City. Revren Lil' Mo Love proclaimed, "Hueynewton, you as bad as Shiftless Rice!"

The next morning Hueynewton and his raggamuffin cabal were right back in the fields. Everyone in town suddenly loved Hueynewton and wanted him to quit the Slavery Experience and stick around to protect them, but Hueynewton wouldn't hear of it. He just couldn't quit early. His ancestors had done a lifetime. The least he could do was a year.

As they picked cotton in the blistering sun, he led them in a blues.

"Swing low, sweet Cadillac," Hueynewton sang.

"Comin for to carry me home!" the others answered.

"Swing low, sweet Cadillac."

"Comin for to carry me home!"

"I looked over Jordan and what did I see?"

"Comin for to carry me home!"

"My Maker's white Cadillac, comin after me."

"Comin for to carry me home."

25

CADILLAC AND Mahogany did not have a good time at King's Flying Youth Basketball tournament. It was at a court in the Raggamuffin Projects, and though the projects were dark, there were large street lamps illuminating everything. Even though it was noon, it looked and felt like late at night. On the court there were all these little boys dunking, and in the stands Mahogany was seven months' pregnant, tired, sweating, grouchy as hell, and so large it seemed the baby was as eager to get out as everyone was to have it out. So many people stared that when people didn't stare it was conspicuous. The *Inquirer* put a picture of her looking fat and pregnant on the cover. As she walked into the park a girl hissed something about the prophecy. Another called her a slut and said she should move to The City. By the end of the game Mahogany would dump him yet again, even though he'd never known that they were a couple. But he was used to that by now.

They'd been spending lots of time together since she'd gotten pregnant, and though they slept together now and then, their time consisted mostly of Mahogany bitching about being pregnant, dying for a cigarette, and making him sprint like a track star turned manservant. She liked having a guy she could push around, who would tolerate her bitchiness, but every morning, when they woke up in her bed, she reminded him that they were not in a relationship. At least once a week she got mad and dumped him.

He was more than willing to run her errands and feed her grapes because he felt terrible that she'd suddenly become an outcast in her own city because of him. But he also had hope that the baby would indeed know how to fly, though she told him constantly that that was impossible. Sometimes he tuned Mahogany out and just admired her beauty without dealing with her ugliness. And he wasn't stupid. There was no sex in the world like flying sex. You, too, would put up with a lifetime of bitchiness to occasionally have flying sex. Thus, they were a young version of those old married couples that love to fight. Wherever they went to eat in town she'd say I fucking hate this place and he would delicately remind her that she'd chosen it, and that it wasn't a bad place after all. He saw Soul City as beautiful and magical. She thought they were a raunchy bunch of strange-acting Negroes a little too happy about being free of The Man. They were both right, and, slowly, they were both learning that.

On the court were little boys in baggy clothes soaring through the air with untied shoelaces dunking though they weren't tall enough to reach the cookies in the cabinet. They walked on air as easily as other boys climb trees, but sometimes you wished they wouldn't.

In the finals King and his friends from Honeypot Hill played the mean boys from Niggatown, who they'd lost to in the finals last year. None of them could shoot, but even if they could've the shots would've had to arc high enough to brush the clouds to avoid being swatted, so they only tried dunks. But they were little boys, so lots of them missed dunks. Boys crashed into each other in midair near the hoop. They'd fall to the concrete and cry over their slightly bloodied knees. One kid tried to dunk and hit his forehead on the rim, got blood all over the place, and had to be taken to the House of Big Mamas. Others made feeble dunks, then hung triumphantly on the rim as they'd seen on TV. It was cute until the end of the first half, when Mahogany's brother missed a dunk that would've given his team the lead and everyone laughed at him because he was her brother.

At halftime Mahogany sat there steaming, upset that she was fat and pregnant, angry that the whole town was mad at her, and furious with Cadillac because he was easy to take it out on. As usual he took all her crap. And then, as the boys came back on the court for the second half, he said, "I love you."

He'd been wanting to say it. She'd been afraid he was wanting to say it.

"OK, that's it," she said. "We're breaking up." She pulled out her cellphone and dialed Carrie Cosmopolitan, the top breakup-ceremony planner in the city.

"I'm gonna show you I mean it this time," she said. "We're gonna have a breakup ceremony."

"I didn't know we were going out."

In the final seconds of the game King took off from the foul line, floated through the lane, and dunked more like a grown man than anyone had all day. His dunk won the game for Honeypot Hill, but nobody cheered for him.

26

O NE DAY around this time, posters appeared throughout Soul City trumpeting the grand opening of the
new Reparations Store on Groove Street. The posters promised a wide variety of reparations options. IT AIN'T JUST 40
ACRES AND A MULE NO MORE! it said. At the bottom was the
name of the proprietor: the Reparations Man. The Soul City
grapevine snapped into action. Who was this stranger in town,
this Reparations Man? Of course, Ubiquity Jones played a
leading role in the detective work that followed.

Those curious enough to make their way over to the Reparations Store found the Reparations Man alone in a tiny office
with just a chair, a desk, and a cheap laptop computer. He was
a caricature of a tiny traveling salesman, with a well-aged
leather briefcase, a tattered tweed jacket, and thick glasses
that he adjusted nervously twice a sentence. He was humble
and yet somehow everyone could tell he was proud of his out-

fit, which was strange for someone in such plain fashion. Most read him as a con man right away and walked out. A few listened to his spiel.

He told all who'd listen that there were only two reparations options available. You could fill out a form, give him a $500 processing fee, and in a week a check for reparations from slavery would arrive from DC signed by the president, The Man, in the amount of $100,000. Or you could buy a Reparations Pill that would instantly clear up any emotional, psychological, philosophical, or spiritual problems related to the lingering impact of slavery. Everyone headed for the door when they heard that snake-oil pitch. Everyone but Ubiquity. She was too curious. She sat through her entire consultation wondering why she couldn't read this man's mind. She'd never met a man whose mind she couldn't read. She knew darn well she wasn't going to get $100,000 from DC. But she also knew the Reparations Man had not moved into town and rented this office just to get her $500. And what if she was wrong and did get $100,000? She signed up for his scam, just to see what the scam was.

When she handed him the cash he said the program required you prove you had a slave ancestor. This would take tremendous work, so he'd done all the genealogical research before coming to Soul City. He opened his computer and found the name of a slave she was related to. She'd never heard of the slave, but she signed the form. The Reparations Man gave her a receipt and told her the check would be in her mailbox within seven business days. Word of Ubiquity's unfortunate investment got around and for a week people snickered behind her back, though quietly, so as not to attract her gossipy wrath. But exactly seven business days after her meeting, a letter arrived from DC, from the office of the president.

Dear Miss Jones,

    I am sorry for what our country has done to you people. Please feel better.

                            Sincerely,
                            The Man

And there was a check for $100,000 signed by The Man. She bounced right over to the Bank of Soul City and deposited it. Then she ran home and called the bank. Before the deposit her account was −$1,000. Now, the computerized voice sounded surprised as it said she had $99,000. Ubiquity thought, I wish I had more slaves in my family. Then she walked around town making sure everyone knew about her slave check. The next day the line to get into the Reparations Store was six blocks long. People wanted their slave check so bad they risked losing their jobs. Some even bought the pills.

But the next day, when Ubiquity called the bank to hear that big number, the computer voice said she had just $68,000. She thought it was a computer error or a virus or something because she certainly hadn't made any purchases, not yet. But the following day the computer voice told her she had only

$31,000. She told herself, it's OK. This is what happens when you're rich. They take money out of your account to give to other people for their withdrawals. They'll put it all back by tomorrow. But when she called the next morning her account had only $9,000, and by the time she got to the bank the teller said her balance was back to −$1,000. The teller said something was indeed strange because he saw the $100,000 deposit and he saw no withdrawals, but somehow her account stood at −$1,000. He said, It's almost as though your money has evaporated. Then he laughed. Ubiquity was furious. She read his mind, then said loud enough for the whole bank to hear, "If you really want to feel sexy you should get out of Victoria's Secret and try La Perla!" Minutes later the poor crossdresser went for a coffee break and never came back to work. He'd been there fifteen years.

Still, Ubiquity was without her money and this would not do. She went back to the Reparations Store, but now the line was twenty blocks and at least five days long. It seemed all of Soul City were becoming slaves to the check. She stormed into the crowded store and interrupted the Reparations Man in the middle of a consultation to tell him that her money had disappeared. He said he knew nothing about the machinations of her bank account and that if she had a problem she should call the one who signed the check. The Man. So, Ubiquity bounced home and did just that. She called the White House and asked to speak to The Man. She thought DC had taken her money back without telling her and she was furious.

She would give The Man a piece of her mind and then read his and get something for the tabloids. Occasionally it worked over the phone.

But Ubiquity got no further than The Man's third assistant secretary, who was unfortunately a woman. She told Ubiquity that her story about a reparations check made no sense because The Man had never and would never sign a reparations check because he didn't believe in reparations. Ubiquity dropped the phone. She'd been fooled. It took quite a lot to fool a mind reader. Who in the hell was this man at the Reparations Store?

When she got to the Reparations Store there was a giant scrum in front of the door with angry people fighting to get in. Seems everyone's $100,000 had disappeared slowly. Even those who'd converted their money to cash had watched that giant stack wither away into thin air. Yet gridlocked within the mob trying to get in and get the Reparations Man, there was a countermob fighting to get in and get their check. Ubiquity couldn't possibly get inside now. But through the glass she could see the Reparations Man reclining in his little chair, seeming thrilled over the chaos he'd caused. Who was this goddam man? She had to alert Fulcrum.

Now, this would take some diplomacy, which Ubiquity lacked. Ubiquity knew that Dream Negro had taken her bomb quite hard. She'd stayed in bed for two weeks and was still quite depressed and embarrassed over her daughter's ongoing bliss problem. Ubiquity tiptoed up to the Negro house, knocked on the door, and painted her biggest, sweetest smile across her face. Dream Negro opened the door, saw Ubiquity and her chins, and ran screaming to her bed. When Fulcrum came out from his office he found his wife babbling and hysterical in bed with all her clothes on. Ubiquity was standing at the door, still smiling brightly. His normally infinite patience immediately reached its end. As he closed the door in her face he heard Ubiquity say something about the strange man at the Reparations Store. Even though no one liked Ubiquity she always, somehow, knew everything. Fulcrum thought, Ubiquity is neither God's most tactful creature nor Her smartest, but she wouldn't bounce her fat ass all the way over here for no reason. He calmed his wife, then took a trip to the Reparations Store.

When Fulcrum got there they were on the verge of a riot. The crowd parted when they saw Fulcrum, who strolled into the store and instantly recognized the humble traveling salesman as the Devil. His costume was quite good, with the tweed jacket and the slightly broken, cheap glasses. You could tell he'd put a lot of time into it. But the quality of the disguise was ruined by the pride with which he wore it, the way he slumped his shoulders to fit the character, but, on a deeper level, seemed to be sticking his chest out like the kid who just knows he's going to win the Halloween contest. It wasn't the costume that gave him away, it was the pride.

The Devil noticed Fulcrum looking at him. Fulcrum couldn't let him know he knew, and the Devil thought his disguise was so good that Fulcrum wouldn't recognize him. So they extended hands and shook and both lied that it was nice to meet you. Fulcrum waited a moment, then hot-stepped out.

The Devil doesn't do long stays on Earth very often because field trips get him really backed up at the office, but after the Jiggaboo fiasco he felt he had to do something. Besides, there was no place on Earth where they enjoyed themselves more than in Soul City, and that burned him. So now he was buying the rights to the souls of various slaves through their relatives. A contact of his at the White House was putting the checks through to The Man, who'd been briefed on the whole scam. The $500 was just so he'd have some throwaway cash, though he had taken special glee in stealing Ubiquity's money. One of the many reasons he'd personally come to Soul City was, in fact, just to steal $500 from her. He really disliked her. (He couldn't wait til she died.) The pills actually worked, but the checks were drawn on The Man's account at the Bank of Hell, meaning you sold your slave ancestor's soul for money that slipped through your fingers. The civic chaos this was causing was a bonus.

As Fulcrum walked down Freedom Ave he had no idea how they could get the Devil out of town quickly. He knew Hueynewton was too tired to face the Devil himself and Shiftless Rice was too old. He couldn't just go around telling people that the Devil was on Groove Street. That would cause pandemonium. Then he saw Big Mama Sweetness Serendipity easing her ancient, mountainous body down the street. He knew exactly what to do.

The next day the Reparations Man got a call from Big Mama Sweetness, who said everyone at the House of Big Mamas wanted their slave check, but they were too old to walk to Groove Street. He said he'd be there half an hour after closing time. Meanwhile, Big Mama Afro was sitting outside the House of Big Mamas. She was 297 years old and four-foot-three, with a fro that was heavier than her entire body because she was the weight of a dry sweater. It wouldn't take long for her little nose to get stuffed up.

An hour later the Reparations Man was sitting on the couch at the House of Big Mamas happily explaining the contract to all the Big Mamas. All save Big Mama Afro, who was kneeling unseen behind the couch, right behind the Reparations Man. The Big Mamas all knew that Death already knew she had a stuffy nose and was at that moment screaming toward the House of Big Mamas. Touching a second Big Mama in under a year would make his century. When Death came through the wall the Devil saw Death zooming right at him and got scared because he thought his disguise was so good that even Death wouldn't recognize him. If Death touched him the next thing he knew he'd be stuck somewhere in the Styx and it took him two days to get home from there, so he ran right out of the House of Big Mamas and went straight back to Hell.

Death kept on racing toward Big Mama Afro, certain he was about to touch her, but he was in a room filled with Big Mamas and he had no chance. One Big Mama gave the signal and Big Mama Afro danced out of the way. Death went flying past her, and when he turned around the Big Mamas were clapping and chanting in a semicircle around Big Mama Sweetness, who was holding Big Mama Afro by the shoulders as if Big Mama Sweetness were a matador with a living, laughing cape. Death ran at them and missed again and again, trying to touch them, trying to end their lives, but he was just a snorting, angry bull for them to tease, their entertainment for the evening. He tried to touch the others but they too danced away, taunting him, teasing him, beating him at his own game, life-and-death tag. Finally, he stopped and whined, "I'm just trying to do my job!" They laughed in his face and showed him the door. Fulcrum was already on his way to Hell to rescue the slaves. Ubiquity tried to write a note of apology to Dream, but she just couldn't do it.

27

ONE NIGHT a few days later Hueynewton was alone in a slave shack, his back aflame from the whipping he'd taken a few hours earlier, watching the world go by without him.

He felt like a prisoner and survived only because he knew he had months left, not a lifetime. He thought of how it would feel to waste your life this way, and a vicarious rage began to boil inside him. Thoughts of whips and chains punctuating his entire life fanned the flames in his heart until a wild fever took hold and he found himself running to The City, running for hours without stopping, straight toward a web he wouldn't get out of.

Jack Hitlerian had been mayor of The City for just a few weeks, but he was already hungry for a nigger to lynch. He'd campaigned on legalizing racial profiling, tripling the police presence in Rhythmtown, building new jails, and generally arresting Black men as quickly and as vaguely as possible. He'd also campaigned with impunity, knowing his opponents didn't dare call him racist because Hitlerian was Black.

In Rhythmtown they saw the glint in his eyes that matched his last name. They felt as if troops were rumbling into their ghetto to herd them off to the camps one by one. They were, but Hitlerian wanted someone else to make the first move. He wanted someone to make it easy on him. He was a spider waiting for someone, anyone, to fall into his web. The night he was elected he promised, "The first nigger who twitches wrong will be made a spectacle!" Others could celebrate the first baby of the year. He looked forward to the first nigger capture of his reign.

Hueynewton was in the middle of The City, looking hard into a sea of white skin, wondering which, if any, of these people came from people who'd owned his. He stared at their faces as if he might remember. The question came again and again and the wild fever ripped at him and yesterday's lash wounds burned anew and his head was filled with Billie's eerie, haunting timbre, wailing about strange fruit. A white man rushing by bumped him. It was one of those crowded city shove-bumps that happen all the time, but after months of the torture of slavery Hueynewton couldn't possibly forgive a white man a single trespass, even a tiny one. He grabbed the man's shoulder, cocked his massive fist, and unloaded in his eye, nearly dislodging it from the socket. Hueynewton stood over him, watching him scrounge in pain on the sidewalk. The police roared in.

When Hueynewton got in the car the charge was felony assault. He thought Emperor would come get him in a few hours. But when they got to the prison hospital one of Hueynewton's eyes was hanging out and three of his ribs were sticking out and the charge was attempted murder of a police officer. There were three witnesses, all of them cops.

As Emperor Jones raced to The City, Mayor Hitlerian told the assembled media that the man who'd brazenly robbed a local KFC just a few months ago was a descendant of Nat Turner and had come to The City for another killing spree, but they'd stopped him before he'd started. The spider had caught a big fly, cocooned him in prison, and was waiting to eat him.

All of Soul City marched and protested for Hueynewton's freedom, but he was too big a trophy to be let go. As the battle stretched on outside, Hueynewton sat in his cell and watched the world going on without him. For him, time stopped. Then one day, his watch stopped. The battery was fine. The watch was being honest. Then pieces of him began flaking from all over his body like leprosy in miniature, or the bit-by-bit crumbling of an ancient, dying statue. Each day another piece flaked off. Each day another person forgot him.

28

As always happened after Mahogany dumped Cadillac, they separated for about a day. After that they would just sort of end up back in each other's world and fall back into the old pattern. Though she dumped him all the time, they never made up, per se, but they never really broke up, either. The week before the breakup ceremony they had dinner three times and slept together twice. But somehow he had a feeling this breakup ceremony was going to be the end of their relationship.

The evening before the breakup ceremony, Cadillac stumbled through the streets of Soul City, drunk and alone. He thought of the sexy DJ he'd met at the Biscuit Shop eight months ago and wished he could have her back. He'd never had her, but that didn't make the upcoming ceremony any less painful. After having drinks at two bars and Lolita, he found his way over to the Hug Shop because, well, he needed a hug.

Ecstasy Jackson was there. He had no idea why everyone always said leave her alone and then laughed. She drove him home in her Curtismobile while Mr. Mayfield spoke about Freddie, who, like him, was dead.

Cadillac was the first man Ecstasy had ever brought to her home in Cloud Nine, where she lived with her mother, MacBeth McGroovy-Jackson, her aunts Saddity McGroovy, Freebush McGroovy, Chloe Wofford, Madamazell Brownberry, and Jambalaya Littlejohn, her great-aunt Irie McGroovy, her granma Honeychile McGroovy, and her busybody seven-year-old half sister, Foin Negro. Their large house, surrounded by weeping willows, was unexpectedly ramshackle considering the upscale neighborhood. It was a patchwork of various woods and aluminums and uneven textures and windows of varying sizes. All sorts of architectural ideas were plastered alongside one another like a giant abstract unsolved Rubik's Cube. The house seemed to be going in thirty-two aesthetic directions because it'd been built over many years by the many men the McGroovy women had had in their lives. Husbands and boyfriends, fiancés and flings — all had come and discovered a houseful of sweet and beautiful women, all ready to dote on any man who dared cross their door. As they fed him and flirted, whispered and worshipped, the men slowly fell in love with the entire lot of them, and, if he was at all inclined, he volunteered to finish the job of working on the house that'd curiously been abandoned by some other guy. As he worked on the house he hung around his girlfriend or wife, fiancée or fling more and more, but it was always too late when he discovered the terrible secret of the McGroovy women: they love too well.

There were no men in the midst of the McGroovys because their men had all been killed, albeit while smiling. Each McGroovy woman, one after the other, fell in love with a man and wooed him til he was hers. They aimed their laser-beam love at him and sometimes he lasted weeks, occasionally months, but no man could survive a McGroovy woman's love, and eventually the raw heat of it would make him simply spontaneously combust. Sometimes at the climax of sex, sometimes during a hug. The boys they birthed ran away as soon as they could.

It was said the McGroovys had earned their freedom from slavery through love. As the story goes, Voodoo McGroovy was enslaved on the Keeprunnin, Mississippi, plantation of Onus McGroovy. When she was just fourteen she sprouted breasts of a shape so robust that Massa Onus found her irresistible. One night he tiptoed out to the slave shacks and had his way with her for two long hours, a session that left her middle and his face very bloody. Soon Massa Onus was down in the shacks bloodying little Voodoo every night, and every morning she prayed the sun would never again set so she could be free of him. She would've given her freedom to escape him, if only it'd been hers to give.

One day, Massa Onus had Voodoo moved from the field to the house, and instead of picking cotton in the sun she was serving meals in the cool with nicer clothes to wear and

Massa's scraps to eat. This did not change her feelings. She still despised him, she just despised him more frequently. After many months of close relations, he fell in love with her and began bringing her little presents, giving her days off, caressing her gently before and after raping her, and letting her get to know him as a man. Love is a flower that blooms in the most arid of deserts, and, somehow, Voodoo began, slowly, to fall in love back. Maybe deep down she knew what would happen.

She stared at him when he entered the room and she lingered in his presence, half hoping he would grab her off into the broom closet, rip open her dress, and have his way with her. She still fought back, she felt she should, but now it was less rape and more rough semiconsensual sex. She didn't wanna want it, but want it she did. It wasn't a love she chose, it was a love that chose her. Well, one night he came to her bed and climbed atop her. But instead of passively allowing a dull, dry entrance, she wettened to his touch and was moved by his rhythm. Instead of clawing into him, she enveloped him. Never in her life had a man's grunt sounded so sweet. And as he rocked above her she crept toward the first and last orgasm of her entire life, and when that explosion finally occurred she felt a love like nothing she'd ever known. She lost all control and screamed out, "Oh, Massa Onus, I LOOOOVES you!" He looked at her in the strangest way, struggling to understand why her words had seemed to unleash a mountain of motion inside his skin. Then he exploded in a million pieces, none larger than a millimeter. Voodoo and several others slipped away that night and beat a path to Soul City.

Now, nearly two centuries later, as Ecstasy introduced Cadillac around the house, Voodoo's great-great-great-grand-daughters MacBeth, Saddity, Chloe, Freebush, Madamazell, and Jambalaya all hoped Ecstasy did not have the family curse. But they were almost certain she did. They all did. They took her aside and told her not to fall in love with this new man, but a McGroovy heart is large and powerful, almost as intoxicating for the lovee as for the lover. So with a mixture of hope and fear, the McGroovy women welcomed Cadillac into their home.

Up in Ecstasy's boudoir there was a tangible tension as the two sat talking long into the night, a cloud of carnal heat engulfing them. Ecstasy fell into a love funk and forgot all about the family curse (which, of course, was part of the family curse). As the hours grew thin the two got horizontal, the grunting grew great, and who arrived but Death, floating in through the window with timing meant to catch the teapot just before it screamed. Death wasn't happy about taking Cadillac's soul across so soon, but no one had forced Cadillac to wander into the web of a black widow of love.

Death knew the sheet-dancing of a McGroovy woman was always an orgy of two of undreamed of erotomaniacal frenzy. But the lust of those two was so electric and athletic that their passion turned him into a peeper. Even though he was impossibly busy, Death turned patient. As Ecstasy's amorousness rose, happy Death got a show, and poor Cadillac, the doomed, cocooned fly looking lovingly at the spider, was moments from a jolt of the unsurvivable McGroovy megakilowatt love and could do nothing for nothing is all he knew. At least, Death thought, his end will be happy. Unbeknownst to all three of them, pressed against the outside of Ecstasy's boudoir door were MacBeth, Saddity, Chloe, Freebush, and Madamazell, who were eager to see her happy, yet feeling they should probably break in and save the poor boy even though that would incur Ecstasy's formidable wrath for the foreseeable future.

The moment was about to arrive. Cadillac was in ecstasy in Ecstasy and her love was just a bit away from boiling and Death, dying to avoid the mess spontaneous combustion always created, reached into his pocket for his Mont Blanc to cross Cadillac off his list as MacBeth bent silently toward the keyhole just trying to get a peek, while her sisters stood stone still around her trying not to freak, but somehow, from outside the boudoir door, came a tiny, little creak. It was Foin. She was supposed to be in bed, but she was kneeling on the floor, looking around the corner, staring at her aunts, not about to let this theater go on without her. Such a nosy busybody. She moved a millimeter and made a noise that broke Cadillac's concentration. He was deeply drunk on Ecstasy's love but somehow experienced a moment of clarity. Mahogany appeared in his mind. He loved her and he would show her in front of all of Soul City. "Stop!" he yelled out. Ecstasy and Death froze and McGroovy ladies of all ages breathed a sigh of relief. "I can't do this," Cadillac said. "I could never love you the way you love me." He had no idea. Later that night around midnight, Mahogany was at home getting ready for the breakup ceremony when there was a buzz at her door. She wasn't expecting anyone. It was Precious.

Nobody'd seen her for months. She was twitching horribly and she seemed to ask for money, but Mahogany couldn't understand her because Precious spoke as if she were deaf. Her eyes were hollow and her face looked sunken as if the life were being sucked out of her from the inside. Her hat was pulled so tight that there were no curves where the ears should've been. You couldn't tell if there were ears there or not.

Mahogany handed Precious some money, but when she reached for it a flake dropped from beneath her hat. They both saw it.

Precious blinked and her eyes were big with tears. She took off her hat. There was nothing left of her ears. They'd withered away flake by flake. Now it looked like there were flat patches of scorched earth on both sides of her head.

29

CADILLAC AND Mahogany's breakup ceremony was held on Saturday, February 13, at the Sunflowers' home, 123 Bluestone Road in Honeypot Hill.

It began at two p.m. The Revren Hallelujah Jones officiated.

More than two hundred people squeezed into Mama Sunflower's backyard for the event. The *Inquirer* had team coverage. Mama Sunflower was shocked to see so many people come to the ceremony. She just knew most of them had never met Mahogany or Cadillac. But she was too thrilled to see the relationship ending to worry about all that. Indeed, more than half the folk at the breakup ceremony didn't know the two. They'd come as if to a public hanging to see the end of this couple that had ruined their lives. But those who actually knew them were sad. Even though she kept dumping him, somehow their dysfunctional nonrelationship worked. The girls from the Biscuit Shop felt those two deserved each other.

Carrie Cosmopolitan, the breakup-ceremony planner, had arranged a very short, simple ceremony. First, the Revren Hallelujah would have thirty seconds to say a few words about Mahogany and Cadillac. Then their friends would have twenty seconds to say a few. Then both Mahogany and Cadillac would get five seconds to state their main gripe with the other, but both had to speak at the same time so neither could say they didn't get the last word. And it was never on the schedule, but at every breakup ceremony there was a fight. With the baby just a month away, the city was tense. The audience at the Sunflowers' that afternoon had the rococo sadism of a crowd at a heavyweight title fight, happily awaiting the violence that would surely arrive at any second.

Cadillac smoothed in to the Sunflower home that afternoon with a secret burning in his pocket. He was either going to win the lottery or get laughed out of town. But he had to try. Flying sex was too good to give up just because she kept dumping him. Besides, to him she was still that sexy DJ who wore Jimmy Choo heels with her Biscuit Shop uniform in the middle of the afternoon. Sure, she had a superiority complex, but if he could fly he'd probably have one, too. At the end of the day, he just loved her. To him, she was the cactus whose milk was so sweet it was worth the needles. If they were gonna have a breakup ceremony he was gonna go down fighting.

Carrie got the Revren, Mahogany, and Cadillac ready to go onstage. Cadillac turned to Mahogany. Without turning her head she said, "Shut up." He did. The Revren, barely five-foot-

two and as fragile as a man made of aluminum foil, turned up
and looked at her with a stare that could stop hearts. He had
baptized Mahogany. The two of them would not make a fool
of him today.

The Revren Hallelujah Jones had given up breakup cere-
monies a few years ago after a particularly gruesome one in
which Amber Sunshower had started a near riot that left
Coltrane Jones with a twice broken left arm. But the good
Revren saw nothing wrong with having the spotlight shine on
him now and again, and Mahogany and Cadillac were a prominent Soul City couple. ("You call them controversial and
tempestuous," the Revren told the *Inquirer*. "I call them mis-
understood.") But he coulda stayed at home if they thought
he'd be the straight man in some madcap slapstick fiasco.
"Behave yo'selves!" he commanded. Then the three moved
onto the little stage.

A moment later, Ubiquity Jones quietly slipped in. She
stood at the back, watching for a glimpse of Cadillac. As soon
as she saw him she read his mind and found he was thinking
about one thing: the surprise. People noticed Ubiquity sashay-
ing on tiptoe over toward Mama Sunflower, but no one dared
say a thing.

The Revren began the ceremony. "We are gathered here
today . . ."

Ubiquity breathed in deeply, calling attention to herself,
announcing less than silently that it was time for a quiet gossip bomb. She whispered just loud enough for Mama Sun-

flower and the ladies around her to hear. "Ain't it a shame she has to watch her daughter marry a boy from *The City?*"

Mama Sunflower didn't turn her head. Everyone knew that voice. Mama whispered, "Girl done lost the sense She gives a baby. This is a *breakup* ceremony and *she* wasn't invited."

The ladies gasped quietly.

"Looks to me," Ubiquity whispered nastily, "like *she* in for a surprise."

The Revren called out, "If anyone has a reason why these two should not break up, speak now or forever hold your peace!"

The city's anger poured out from the crowd. Someone yelled, "City boy!" Then someone screamed, "Fly away, Judas!" Mama Sunflower looked ashen. It seemed the whole world was against them. Then Cadillac stepped to the center of the stage.

"I know this baby will fly," he said to her as the yelling went on around them. "But even if it can't, I'd still love you." He got down on one knee and pulled out a robin's-egg-blue box that said TIFFANY. All of Soul City gasped. He popped the question, then opened the box. There was a little rainbow trapped inside.

Mahogany turned away immediately. There was no way she could look at it. She was tired though she'd just woken up, the baby was kicking like crazy, and her Jimmy Choos were killing her. But she was impressed that he'd risked extraordinary public humiliation for her. She realized he'd stuck by her through everything. That he couldn't ruin her life any more than he already had. And having a man she could boss around forever was not bad at all. Then she peeked at the ring. It was a two-carat nugget. *It's huge,* she thought. And then her icy heart began to melt. She did love him. She'd fought so hard against it, but he was the lid to her pot. She didn't wanna want it, but want it she did. It wasn't a love she chose. It was a love that chose her.

And so Mahogany Sunflower finally decided to give Cadillac Jackson a chance. She looked down at him and said, "Maybe."

The crowd went wild as if they'd seen a surprise knockout. But they weren't sure who'd won. For anyone else *maybe* would've been crushing. But for Cadillac at that moment with that woman, *maybe* was victory enough. He stood and Mahogany leaned in and gave him a kiss on the mouth. A brief, closed-mouth kiss of like. Like that could blossom. Maybe.

Ubiquity crowed as she bounced out the door. The ladies looked at Mama Sunflower with pity. She'd been bombed by her daughter and her nemesis in her own home at the same time. But Mama Sunflower still would not break. She was too curious. How could Ubiquity have possibly known?

Mahogany and Cadillac began dating officially and almost nothing changed. They went right back to being a youngish old married couple that fights all the time. Mahogany complained and bossed him around, but she didn't dump him once a week anymore.

As Mahogany's ninth month approached Soul City grew increasingly nervous over what would happen to them after the baby was born. The Big Mamas didn't know. No one expected an instant apocalypse, but what were they headed for?

Fulcrum went to Heaven.

All She would say is, "Have faith."

And the entire city sat on the edge of its seat waiting for this baby to come.

30

_____

ON THE first day of her ninth month it rained so horribly people said another flood was coming, thanks to Mahogany. The couple stayed in her apartment all day. They didn't go out anymore. People on the street said the nastiest things. The whole city was watching, but they felt alone. Even if the prophecy had been fake, by now it had become real. The city was so tense that if that baby didn't fly it would indeed be the end of Soul City as they knew it. And there was no way the baby would be able to fly.

Mahogany was so nervous she almost smoked. Only Cadillac's faith buoyed her. She demanded they have the baby at home. It was due in three weeks, but as they'd find out, that baby would always do everything when it was good and ready.

That afternoon Cadillac was making yet another attempt to construct the perfect first sentence for his book. Once he had the perfect first sentence he knew the rest would trickle out a drop at a time over many excruciating years, but at least the suffering would've begun. He thought of Márquez, Rushdie, and Ellison at their desks, struggling to bring life to Macondo, Bombay, and Harlem. He would keep fighting until he found the perfect first sentence.

Then the baby let Mahogany know it was good and ready, coming three weeks early, as if it, too, could no longer stand the anticipation. Cadillac called the midwife and she started on her way, but in the heavy rain she got into an accident and died. Now they were really alone.

A little foot popped out. The midwife wasn't answering her cell and Mahogany was speaking in tongues, so Cadillac began gently tugging on the foot, trying to help the baby come out. Three hours later, the gentle tugging had become a tug of war, the room was exactly as wet and as wild as if the biblical rain outside was falling inside the apartment, there was blood and birth juice everywhere, and he could see only half of the baby, but enough to know she was having his son. His little hips gave Cadillac more to pull on. But then the boy stopped coming. He was more than halfway out, they were almost done, but his head was trapped, the cord wrapped around his neck. His little face was starting to turn blue. Mahogany ordered Cadillac to wait for the midwife. Certainly, she would arrive any second. He thought that was wise. But, full of hope, he reached in. Slowly, delicately, Cadillac eased the cord aside and smoothed his son out.

"I can't believe we did this at home," she said as he cut the cord.

He did not remind her that that'd been her choice.

Hero Jackson began his life not by flying but by falling asleep in his mother's arms as if he, too, were tired from the expectations. Cadillac and Mahogany stared at the wrinkled little creature, too in love to worry about anything. Hero slept for twenty minutes and then, with his mother's sense of nonchalance about the amazing and his own need to do things when he was good and ready, he yawned. Then he lazily lifted up into the air. He was a little brown Baryshnikov, gliding backwards in the air as if to say, *Of course I can fly.* Then he landed in the arms of his mother. His shocked, relieved, proud mother. Then all three of them melted with the ardor that's possible only with brand-new love.

They would never know that for the first twenty minutes of his life Hero Jackson was unable to fly. He hadn't gotten the flight gene, just as she'd known he wouldn't. But Soul City needed that baby to fly, and when it really matters She always comes through for Soul City.

31

———

A YEAR LATER they got married. The ceremony was held at the Sunflowers' home. More than three hundred were invited to come cheer on what was suddenly Soul City's favorite couple. Mama Sunflower fell in love with those two the moment she saw her grandchild fly.

The Revren Hallelujah Jones officiated. King Sunflower flew in with the ring. The girls from the Biscuit Shop served as maids of honor. Fulcrum and Granmama watched together in Heaven. Jiggaboo watched from Hell. "A nigger who sticks by his girl when the chips are down?" he said to the Devil. "Now *that's* magic realism." The Revren Lil' Mo Love diddled Miss Delicate Chocolate in the closet. Lolita handled the catering and sent three of their top people: Invisible Man was the manager because he was a good thinker and a good leader, Janie Crawford from *Their Eyes Were Watching God* was a bartender because she was always a good worker, Irie Jones from *White Teeth* was a waiter, and Doc Craft from the legendary "A Solo Song: For Doc" absolutely had to be there because he was a Waiter's Waiter. And Emperor Jones took a break from his duties as interim mayor and DJ'd the event. The Sunflower backyard rocked until five in the morning. The *Inquirer* was not allowed in, so they hovered above in a helicopter.

Cadillac was so happy he smoked half a box of Cubans by himself.

Mahogany was tired, dying for a cigarette, so pregnant she was showing, and constantly complaining about how her Jimmy Choos were killing her. But she smiled all day.

Hero didn't cry once during the service in which his parents jumped over the antebellum broomstick used in all Soul City weddings for more than a century. But no one could keep the rambunctious and stubborn boy from flying over to the DJ booth. Some said, He's just like his mother. Others said, Maybe he'll be mayor someday.

Ubiquity Jones was, of course, not invited. She'd let it be known that she was determined to make Chickadee Sunflower cry. But Mama had a bomb of her own. She'd gotten a hunch, made some long-distance calls, and uncovered Ubiquity's secret. She was *hoping* Ubiquity came. She told the guards, If she comes, let her right in.

True to form, Ubiquity slinked in during dinner and hid in the back. She must've had a whopper of a bomb to drop because when she bounced up to the microphone she said,

"Eve-nin, *Soul City!*" She'd come to ruin everyone's night. "Ain't it a *shaaame . . . !*" she sang out with rare glee and the entire city braced itself for a nuclear gossip bomb.

Then Mama Sunflower stood and began walking toward her with one thought in her head. Ubiquity turned to Mama and read her mind and found her own secret. She was horrified. She couldn't have everyone know. That would never do. So as Mama stared her down, Ubiquity backed away from the microphone and quickly bounced to the door. Without a word Mama Sunflower had made Ubiquity Jones run and cry.

32

NOW, MANY years later, Cadillac and Mahogany are an old married couple that fights all the time. But they're happy. One Sunday morning they were at a café in Honeypot Hill. Stevie was on the city speakers talking about paradise when she took a drag and said, "I hate this place." Cadillac didn't have to remind her that she'd chosen it, but he did ask if there was someplace she'd rather be. They could move to The City, Paris, Jamaica, wherever she chose. She was offended. "I would never leave Soul City," she said coldly. She loved her hometown. But she loved complaining, too. She would've hated paradise.

Cadillac became a columnist at the *Soul City Defender*. Mahogany used her reputation as Soul City's best babysitter to launch a day-care center. It was very successful and now she also owns the Biscuit Shop. She still DJs on Friday nights and they still don't have cornbread. They have two children,

Hero and their daughter, Diva. They all live in a nice house on Juneteenth Boulevard in Honeypot Hill. After considerable argument, they bought a Marleymobile because it's a great family car. They still have great flying sex, and though it doesn't always seem so, they love each other.

After his term as interim mayor ended, Emperor Jones ignored the pleas of his doctors and girlfriends and ran for reelection. He won easily and held office for twenty years until the night he died in the DJ booth. He was ninety-four.

Precious Negro kicked bliss and got new hi-tech ears.

Fulcrum Negro reluctantly got Lizzie Benzman a temporary furlough from Hell.

Revren Lil' Mo Love only got cuter as he got older. At eighteen he ran off to Hollywood. He now gets $10 million a picture. He never finished the Bible.

King Sunflower is in the NBA. He's a three-time slam-dunk champ.

Ubiquity promised Mama she'd never reveal a secret again if Mama would keep hers. Mama never would've told Ubiquity's secret. That wasn't her style. But she made the deal anyway.

One day, many years after moving to Soul City, Cadillac was washing the dishes when he noticed his neighbor Miss Delicate Chocolate's garden was half roses and half weeds, but still beautiful because in Soul City even the weeds had style. He thought if he could write a sentence that included Soul City's magic roses and its soulful weeds, he might have a sentence that would encapsulate Soul City. All these years he still hadn't written a word of his book because he was afraid of getting it wrong and being branded a fool or getting it too right and being branded a traitor. He couldn't possibly do a simplistic celebration of these complex folk. He knew too much. But he was afraid to reveal everything he knew and felt about Soul City. In the grasp of the claws of fear you can't hit a jump shot and you certainly can't write. If he was going to talk about these complex folk, he'd have to tell all he saw.

He turned himself into a camera and framed Soul City as he saw it. He said a prayer as he began, for he knew not where his book would end, but he'd lived there for so many years he was one of them. He hoped they would know that even though it wouldn't always be pretty, it would be a love letter.

He picked up his pen and wrote a sentence:

In Soul City they so bad they got beautiful ways of bein ugly.

Finally, he was on his way.

After that the book came to him in slow drips. There were long droughts and ten excruciating years in which he nearly lost his mind, but he soldiered on until one day, thirty-three years after he smoothed off the train, Cadillac finally published *Soul City*.

Some called him honest, others called him a Judas. Some considered him an artist, others compared him to Fetchit. But he slept well at night because never once in the writing did he lie to himself.

Hero grew up to become mayor. In fact, he was widely thought to be the best mayor Soul City had ever had until Ecstasy's little sister, Foin, started to like him and Ubiquity uncovered a secret she couldn't keep to herself and Death finally found a PR agent smart and powerful enough to help him. He told her he'd been feared too long. Now he just wanted to be loved. The crusade to change Death's global image was launched with a book titled *Don't Be Afraid, It's Just Death,* a tell-all about dying that demystified the whole thing and apologized for centuries of fear and misunderstanding. Then he did the talk-show circuit. The book was an immediate monster bestseller, bigger than even the Bible. The demystification of death brought so much relief to so many that Death came to be loved around the world. In time he removed all fear of dying, which had the unintended effect of changing everyone's relationship with God, which led to a mass worldwide conversion to a brand-new religion called Coolism. But that's a story for another day.

Thank You

Mom, Dad, Dr. Meika, Rita, Minna Proctor, Nelson George, Sarah Lazin, Michael Pietsch, Reagan Arthur, Claire McKinney, Stanley Crouch, Eddie Lintz, Stephen Koch, il Bogliasco Fondzatione, and the wonderful Rockhouse Hotel in Negril, Jamaica.

Also, Pryor, Bearden, Ellison, Nabokov, Rushdie, Didion, Hurston, Morrison, García Márquez, David Foster Wallace, Grass, Rand, Amis, Zadie, Amanda Davis, Basquiat, Mary Jane, the word *nigga*, and, of course, the people of Soul City.

Soul City was written in Montauk, New York; Bogliasco, Italy; Negril, Jamaica; and Brooklyn, New York.

About the Author

Touré is the author of *The Portable Promised Land,* a collection of short stories from Little, Brown. He's also a contributing editor at *Rolling Stone,* the host of MTV2's *Spoke N' Heard,* and a contributor to CNN. His writing has appeared in *The New Yorker,* the *New York Times, Tennis Magazine, The Best American Essays 1999, The Best American Sports Writing 2001, Da Capo Best Music Writing 2004,* and *The Best American Erotica 2004.* He studied at Columbia University's graduate school of creative writing and lives in Fort Greene, Brooklyn. (www.Toure.com)